W9-BSC-085

HE DREW HER CLOSER—

"I'm beginning to think you need this more than I do. . . . Relax, Amanda." Ignoring her struggles, he bent his head to kiss the side of her neck and then trailed his lips along her soft skin.

Amanda was agonizingly aware of his every movement and when his hands moved caressingly down her back, her body quivered in response. Then all her resistance collapsed; her arms went around his neck as she closed her eyes and her lips blindly sought his. He was right! *This was what she had wanted all along. . . .*

Other SIGNET Books by Glenna Finley

☐ **BRIDAL AFFAIR** (#Q5962—95¢)

☐ **JOURNEY TO LOVE** (#T4324—75¢)

☐ **KISS A STRANGER** (#Q6175—95¢)

☐ **LOVE IN DANGER** (#Q6177—95¢)

☐ **LOVE'S HIDDEN FIRE** (#Q6171—95¢)

☐ **LOVE LIES NORTH** (#Q6017—95¢)

☐ **LOVE'S MAGIC SPELL** (#Q6022—95¢)

☐ **A PROMISING AFFAIR** (#Q5855—95¢)

☐ **THE ROMANTIC SPIRIT** (#Q5577—95¢)

☐ **SURRENDER MY LOVE** (#Q5736—95¢)

☐ **TREASURE OF THE HEART** (#Q6090—95¢)

☐ **WHEN LOVE SPEAKS** (#Q6181—95¢)

THE NEW AMERICAN LIBRARY, INC.,
P.O. Box 999, Bergenfield, New Jersey 07621

Please send me the SIGNET BOOKS I have checked above.
I am enclosing $_____(check or money order—no
currency or C.O.D.'s). Please include the list price plus 25¢ a
copy to cover handling and mailing costs. (Prices and numbers are subject to change without notice.)

Name_____

Address_____

City_____State_____Zip Code_____
Allow at least 3 weeks for delivery

The Reluctant Maiden

by
Glenna Finley

A SIGNET BOOK
NEW AMERICAN LIBRARY
TIMES MIRROR

COPYRIGHT © 1975 BY GLENNA FINLEY

All rights reserved

 SIGNET TRADEMARK REG. U.S. PAT. OFF. AND FOREIGN COUNTRIES
REGISTERED TRADEMARK——MARCA REGISTRADA
HECHO EN CHICAGO, U.S.A.

SIGNET, SIGNET CLASSICS, MENTOR, PLUME AND MERIDIAN BOOKS
are published by The New American Library, Inc.,
1301 Avenue of the Americas, New York, New York 10019

FIRST PRINTING, JANUARY, 1975

1 2 3 4 5 6 7 8 9

PRINTED IN THE UNITED STATES OF AMERICA

*Maids' nays are nothing: they are shy
But do desire what they deny.*

—HERRICK

Chapter One

A chime sounded softly in the cabin of the airplane before the brisk announcement from the flight deck. "Ladies and gentlemen, we are starting our descent for Mexico City and are anticipating an arrival at their International Airport approximately twelve minutes from now. Please fasten your seat belts and refrain from smoking at this time."

The message was repeated in Spanish and then the overhead lights switched on again as the microphone clicked off. Simultaneously, the sound of the engines changed to a different pitch as the sleek Boeing jet headed for landing after the three-hour flight from Los Angeles.

Amanda Stewart pushed a strand of hair back from her cheek and sighed as she peered through the plane window at her side. Unfortunately, the thick cloud cover beneath the wings refused to part. After clear weather in Baja California at the beginning of their flight, smoke from scattered forest fires over the inland mountains had mingled with smog to blank out all glimpses of the ground for the last hour. As Amanda stared at the gray swirling mass below, she hoped sincerely that the view meant more to the pilot than it did to her.

Finally, she turned back again and reached for her

purse on the seat beside her, taking out her compact to stare somberly into its small, round mirror.

There was no reason for such a solemn appraisal; her nose was short and straight and needed only a little powder to restore its usual mien. The pair of eyes staring back at her were the soft brown of honeyed amber framed by thick lashes of the same shade. Her hair was slightly lighter with sandy streaks in it after exposure to the California sun. It was pulled back in a chignon at her nape—but the simple style effectively emphasized the classical outline of her features. Amanda, however, saw only the shiny nose and frowned as she smoothed the collar of her dress.

Just then the plane hit a bad air pocket and lurched alarmingly. Her startled gaze went back to the window and she discovered the cloud cover had parted, revealing Mexico's capital city spread out beneath them. When the plane banked sharply in the landing pattern, the pyramids of Teotihuacán loomed up to the north, their geometric shapes looking like oversized building blocks on the flat plain. Amanda caught her breath in delight, and an airline steward paused by her seat to ask, "First visit to Mexico City?"

Amanda shook her head. "No . . . I came down on a Christmas holiday some years ago but I'd forgotten how impressive those pyramids were."

"If you like pyramids, you should visit Yucatán." The man's glance flicked admiringly over her delicate cheekbones. "It isn't difficult to get there—even if you are traveling alone."

Amanda's chin went up at that. "I won't be traveling alone. I'm being met in Mexico City."

"I see." He matched her impersonal tone. "Well, I hope you have a pleasant holiday. Please remain

seated until we are at the terminal, Miss Stewart."
He continued down the aisle, obviously dismissing
her from his mind.

Amanda wished that she could have done the
same. Until that exchange, she had successfully
shoved the prospect of meeting Christopher Jarrow to
the back of her mind. She shot an annoyed look at
the empty seat by her side and wondered for the
umpteenth time since they'd taken off how he'd had
the nerve to stand her up.

She had fidgeted in the Los Angeles air terminal
until boarding time for the flight and then frantically called her publisher in New York. "He isn't
here," she had announced as soon as the connection
came through. "What in the dickens do I do now?"
Then without giving her employer a chance to answer, she had added bitterly, "I *told* you it wouldn't
work. That man would stoop to anything to get even
with me!"

"My dear Amanda," he interrupted, "since this is a
collect call, could I possibly get a word in edgewise."

"You already have or I wouldn't be standing here
now. Look ... what do I do? I'm supposed to be
boarding the plane and I haven't seen a sign of
him."

"I'm trying to tell you," her employer spoke with
the patience of long acquaintance. "Chris won't be
there. He called from Mexico City a little while ago
to say he'd taken an earlier flight." At her angry
gasp, he went on hurriedly, "Just get on your plane.
Chris will meet you at the hotel down there later
tonight."

"Do you mean to tell me that after I flew all the
way out here from New York, he couldn't bother to
keep the appointment? And *now* I'm supposed to tag

after him to Mexico City ... when I could have flown directly there in the first place?"

"He *did* apologize. Apparently something came up."

"I'll bet!" Her sarcasm was withering. "And if I know Mr. Jarrow, she was a simpering brunette who doesn't know one end of the alphabet from the other. I remember his tastes ..."

"He said that he was sure you'd understand." There was an undercurrent of laughter from the other end of the wire.

Amanda took a tighter grip on the receiver. "Look," she said aloud. "This simply won't work. I *told* you it wouldn't. Chris Jarrow and I can't be in the same state without disagreeing—let alone the same hotel. You'll *never* get another book out of him with me as his editor. I'm surprised he didn't head for China instead of Mexico!"

"Since the book's on Yucatán—that would be the hard way."

"Detouring by Disneyland on the way from Manhattan to Mexico City doesn't make sense either. Maybe the idiot owns stock in the airlines——"

"Speaking of airplanes," her employer interrupted, "I'd suggest you board *that* one. You know damned well how tight the schedule is in Yucatán. Chris can't afford to hang around waiting for you in Mexico City."

"Honestly—you haven't listened to a word I said ..."

"Yes, I have, and don't try sending in your resignation from there. I'll come down and make you eat it piece by piece if you do. Be a good girl—and bury the hatchet with Chris."

"I'd like to. Right between his ears."

"That's the spirit. You always do your best work

when you're in a temper. Give my regards to him. 'Bye, Amanda."

She heard the sound of a click in her ear and slammed down her own receiver. Turning, she saw the airline ticket agent doing an angry semaphore to get her attention. She bit her lip with irritation, scooped up her purse and started to run—sliding through the boarding door just before the attendant closed it.

From their takeoff to the final glimpse of Baja California, she had sat in her seat and steamed over Chris Jarrow's newest peccadillo. Actually, she told herself, she should have expected such a thing. Since the man had juggled careers as a successful novelist and history professor for the first thirty-three years of his life, he wasn't a meek and mild creature waiting to be led around. Especially when it involved his new manuscript on Yucatán. Even now, it was being publicized as a lead title for the forthcoming season and the only person who wasn't excited about its possibilities was Chris Jarrow himself. "Why on earth didn't we request a firm delivery date when he signed the contract?" Amanda had asked her boss some weeks before when her questioning letters about the manuscript's arrival had brought no response.

"Because he didn't want to sign a contract at all," she was told. "He even haggled over the advance— the guy isn't human."

"I could have told you that," Amanda retorted bitterly. "He must have stacks of my letters by now. All unopened."

"What about telephoning?"

"He had the phone disconnected. I tell you the creature does it deliberately. He gets a sadistic pleasure out of ignoring me."

"That's ridiculous. Why does he insist on having

you for an editor then? He came right out and said that he won't work with anybody else. You must have the whammy on him." Her chief peered across the desktop at her. "What happened out there in Los Angeles when you edited that first book of his?"

"Nothing happened—I keep telling you. But I'm sorry now I didn't push him out the window when I had the chance." Amanda had stormed out of the office, knowing very well that he didn't believe her.

Which wasn't surprising, as it wasn't exactly true.

As the plane moved down through the cloud layers, Amanda stared blindly out of the window and remembered another day five months before at the same Los Angeles airport.

The flight for her return to New York had already been called when Chris came striding into the boarding area and thrust an armful of red roses at her, much to the pleased amusement of her fellow passengers who welcomed the development as something to brighten their boredom.

"I never thought I'd make it . . ." Chris was breathing hard. "I've been trying to find a parking space for the last fifteen minutes. Damned if I wasn't ready to leave it in a bus zone."

"Chris, these roses are beautiful," Amanda stuttered, wondering what had gotten into him to bring about such a change in manner. Generally his actions were performed with an enviable economy of movement.

She surveyed his thin face wonderingly—letting her gaze wander over his firm jawline and linger as it encountered his intelligent glance. Those gray eyes had watched her changing behavior dispassionately for the past month but now there was a disturbing gleam in their depths. His dark hair was falling over his forehead and she had to stifle an impulse to reach up and push it back . . . as she had stifled other impulses during the time they had been together. She stared at his long, lanky frame, wishing that he had looked at her that way when they'd had their farewell dinner in Monterey the night before. Not now, when it was too late. When she had his revised manuscript in her briefcase.

She blinked rapidly and buried her nose in the bouquet of fragrant flowers. "You shouldn't have . . ." she muttered incoherently. "Long-stemmed roses cost a fortune. It was terribly nice of you but——"

He paid no attention, cutting in ruthlessly. "Listen, Amanda, I don't want you to go. I know I shouldn't have left it till now but I just figured out a little while ago that I've fallen in love with you. Up until this morning, I thought the feeling would go away, but it doesn't. It gets worse all the time." He stared down at her in some irritation.

"Oh, Chris . . ." she stood there quivering, uncertain whether to laugh or cry. "You don't have to make it sound like an attack of the flu, for heaven's sake."

He managed a lopsided grin. "The symptoms are the same. I've certainly gone down for the count."

"I don't believe it. Do you know that you haven't even held my hand in the four whole weeks we've worked together? I felt like somebody's maiden aunt."

"It was safer that way," he admitted. "And you know damned well that you couldn't look like a maiden aunt if you tried, my girl. Use your head."

Since masculine attention had spilled over Amanda from age seventeen—a common occurrence for brown-eyed blondes with the proper measurements—she knew he had a point. "Well, I was beginning to wonder if I should change my perfume or dye my hair." Her eyes flashed. "Honestly, Chris, how *could* you! Ignoring me when I've been positively flirting with you for the last two weeks. You could have at least kissed me good night once or twice."

"If I had, I'd never have gotten around to leaving," he told her flatly. "You aren't the type for anything but a wedding ring, and I didn't plan to get married for another five years." He grinned then. "I didn't know that you'd already managed to rearrange my life."

"I didn't. I merely edited your manuscript," she protested weakly as he moved closer.

"I should know. Look, honey—we can catch a plane to Las Vegas and be married this afternoon. I have a terrific idea for a honeymoon . . ." The thought prompted him to abandon rational arguments and he gathered her in his arms . . . roses and all.

His kiss was all that Amanda had ever hoped and dreamed it would be. When they eventually drew apart, it was only long enough to catch their breath before hungrily reaching for each other again.

Amanda had to cling weakly to Chris's jacket for support when he finally released her. He stared down at her, equally bemused. Then he took her hand in proprietary fashion, "Come on, dearest—let's go. We can have your bags sent on."

Sanity returned to Amanda with the shock of a cold shower. "But, Chris darling—I can't," she'd wailed. "Be sensible. I have to get this manuscript back to New York to meet the printer's deadline. Besides"—she reached up and touched a hesitant finger to his cheek—"you can't be serious. A woman needs time when she gets married. In a month or so, I can make plans and take some time off. By then, my job will have settled down."

Chris lowered his hands slowly from her waist. "You really mean that, don't you?" he said finally with a penetrating look. "You're right, of course. You'd better get on the plane." He urged her toward the door, pausing to pick up a rose which had fallen from her arms.

"Just a minute." Her eyes had widened at his casual tone. "I don't understand." She lowered her voice as she suddenly noticed the interested audience around them. "For a second there, I thought I'd heard a proposal."

"Oh, you did." He was pushing her toward the ramp. "There's no need for your father to get out the shotgun. But since you turned me down . . ."

"I *didn't* turn you down." She stopped and shook his hand from her elbow. "I just said that we had to be sensible and wait until . . ."

". . . We're both in the mood," he finished in his normal laconic tones. "Damned good idea. After you get back to New York—let me know when you're ready . . ."

An incredible feeling of relief poured over her until she heard his next words.

". . . Then I'll let you know if I am," he continued. "That certainly makes more sense. Agreed?"

She had stared at him as if she couldn't believe her ears. "You're not serious?"

For a second there was a flicker of anger in his glance. Then it turned blandly opaque again. "Of course I am. You're hard to please. What's wrong with that idea?"

"Well, it's certainly not very romantic."

"You're right—but coming in second to a lousy manuscript won't make the late show either. I'll have to improve my technique. Too bad we couldn't get in any more practice."

Amanda flushed as she looked up at his tight features. "It's better we didn't. You know darn well there isn't a thing wrong with your technique." She paused by the ramp, wondering what she'd do if he simply ignored her objections and hauled her into his arms again.

Unfortunately, she didn't have the chance to find out. Chris merely smiled at the passing stewardess before saying, "Well, good-bye, Amanda. Work hard and let me know what your plans are."

"I'll make a note of it." She decided she could be as nasty as he was. "Just as soon as I have a minute."

"Do that." He sketched a casual farewell. "I'll be in touch."

On that flight, it had taken her about two minutes to realize that she'd been a full-fledged idiot. Since it was a nonstop plane she couldn't transfer at the next airport and she had to settle for apologizing when he called. She would tell him she was available for a wedding ceremony any time he chose. Also that she loved him quite desperately. As they crossed the California border, she realized she'd forgotten to mention that fact, as well.

She waited for his phone call all the next day. Later in the week, she even went home on her lunch hour to see what was in her mailbox—hoping to find a scrawled postcard saying, "Let's stop this nonsense, Amanda. Come back, I can't live without you."

All the mailbox offered was the usual stack of bills and an advertisement for a circular dog house.

The third week she shed four pounds because she'd lost her appetite. On the fourth, she swallowed her last bit of feminine pride and wrote Chris a polite note revealing that things were very quiet in the publishing business just then and it was a good thing she didn't take her career seriously.

Her letter was returned, unopened, with a covering note from Chris's apartment manager. Mr. Jarrow, he wrote, had left three weeks ago for an extended trip to South America to study the headwaters of the Amazon. The exact date of his return would probably be in about six months. If she would care to make a note of it . . .

At first, Amanda was so stricken she could hardly move. Then after the words sank in, her strength returned along with her temper. Chris must have had a hand in that! Probably he had left instructions for the man, knowing that she would weaken first.

She tore up both letters with trembling fingers. Damn the man! Making a proposal and then going off to the other end of the world while she cooled her heels! She'd show him! He could spend the rest of his life ten feet *under* the headwaters of the Amazon if she had her way . . . preferably waters infested with schools of piranhas thirsting for blood.

The next day she had resolved to wash her hands of the whole affair. As far as the male sex was concerned, she was now a far wiser woman. No man would ever find her so vulnerable again!

It was sheer bad luck that five months later, Mr. Jarrow wheeled into her orbit again. Not only had he successfully evaded all the dangers of the river—he had the effrontery to demand her presence on his new book. Probably to demonstrate personally how well he had gotten along without her.

After trying futilely to escape from the assignment, she had given in without revealing the true reason for her reluctance. The interval since she'd seen Chris had enabled her to construct a thick wall around her emotions, and the chip on her shoulder was high enough to wobble in the wind. When she boarded the plane for Los Angeles, the battle cry of trumpets rang on the horizon, only to turn into discord five hours later.

Chris had thwarted her again; the big dramatic climax had sputtered and fizzled. Like a daytime soap opera, it was to be continued in the next installment.

Another moment of turbulence as the plane banked for its final approach to the long runway at Mexico City roused Amanda from her apathy. Then the big jet landed fast on the high altitude strip and a few minutes later was taxiing back to the terminal. Amanda unfastened her seat belt and heaved a sigh of relief. Cross-continent flights were not her cup of tea, she decided. If only she didn't have to meet Chris right away. A few hours' sleep would put her in better shape for the encounter. Now—after her cross-country commuting—she was too drained to fight back.

Fortunately, the immigration and customs formalities were quickly handled. After her tourist card was stamped and signed, the Mexican customs man merely eyed her luggage on the counter and genially waved her on toward the waiting porter. Within minutes, Amanda was capably stowed in a cab and on her way back to the city center.

Her arrival was on the fringe of the rainy season, but the humid air felt thick enough to slice and already her dress was clinging to her shoulders. The parklike strip separating the wide street was crowded with city-dwellers determined to enjoy any chance of an outdoor breeze. Some strolled on the grassy strip, other couples sat on the ground either talking or nuzzling each other affectionately . . . depending on their age. One middle-aged woman was calmly knitting her way through an afghan as she sat on the grass.

Music spilled out of eating places and corner bars where large signs extolled the glories of Mexican beer. A hot dog stand took the positive approach, advertising *"Exquisitos Calientitos."* Amanda's stomach thought it over and rumbled warningly.

She felt a moment of panic. It must be the altitude, she told herself. All she needed was a nice quiet hotel room. A nice quiet air-conditioned hotel room. The last amenity was tacked on hastily as the cab turned off the Avenida Juarez and pulled up under an imposing building marquee.

She staggered out of the car when a young bellboy came running from the lobby. By that time, her dress felt as if it had been pasted to her back and she could feel the limp tendrils of her hair clinging to her neck. At least there was no one she knew to see her bedraggled state, she told herself as she paid off the cabdriver.

"Pero, senorita ... diez pesos ... no tip." The bald-headed cabdriver's wail of anguish stopped her on the hotel steps and arrested even the bellhop's movement.

"Senorita, the driver wants more money ..." he confirmed in ringing tones.

"Everybody pays tip ..." the cabdriver howled, pleased with his success. He waved his arms toward the startled passersby. *"Es necessario—si?"*

"Maybe five more pesos," the bellboy offered.

Amanda searched her wallet frantically. "But I don't *have* pesos. I don't have any change at all."

An enterprising young man who had been watching from the sidewalk took advantage of the confusion and sidled up to her. "How about a watch,

instead, lady? All good Swiss makes . . . take a look."
He shoved out his arm toward her, exhibiting sam-
ples from wrist to elbow. "Very cheap. Very good
prices . . ."

"I *have* a watch," Amanda said, disconcerted by
the new attack. "I just need some change."

"Maybe for your husband . . . a special price . . ."

"I don't have a husband."

"Your lover, maybe?"

"I don't have a . . . oh, for heaven's sake . . . *will*
you go away!" She tried to ignore the circle of on-
lookers as she turned back to the cabdriver. "If you
could just wait a minute," she began and then, at his
outraged expression, changed to faltering Spanish,
"*Un momento, por favor, senor.* Oh, lord, how do
you say, 'I don't have any change.'?"

"*No tengo cambiar,*" replied a bored voice behind
her.

"*No tengo cambiar,*" Amanda parroted faithfully.

"Did you know that you're blocking the entrance?"

"Did you know that you're blocking . . ." she continued until the words sank in. Startled, she turned
to see Chris Jarrow, immaculate in a light gray summer suit, surveying her with disdainful amusement.
Her heart sank to her shoe-tops as his gaze swept
over her slowly—not missing a single untidy feature
en route.

"Go on into the lobby while I take care of this
mess," he said finally.

She opened her lips to protest—to say that she just
needed five pesos to tip the man—that she wasn't in a
mess at all. Then she gave a sigh of resignation and
started in the door.

"Oh . . . Amanda . . ."

She winced and looked back over her shoulder.
"Yes?"

"I just wanted to say—Welcome to Mexico."

"Thanks. Thanks very much." Blindly, Amanda turned back toward the safety of the lobby.

It was quite possible, she thought bitterly, that Cortez and Montezuma had exchanged a similar greeting just before the Aztec leader lost his head.

Chapter Two

Evidently Chris felt Amanda was capable of finding the front desk of the hotel and registering because she saw no sign of him while she completed the formalities and then followed a bellboy to an immaculate room on the ninth floor. It featured a queen-sized bed and contemporary furniture with floor-to-ceiling windows overlooking the busy Avenida Juarez and a pleasant park beyond.

"This is very nice," Amanda said after the bellboy had arranged her bags on the luggage racks and checked the bathroom light. She tried to tip him as he handed her the key but he shook his head.

"Senor Jarrow ... he paid after he fixed the taxi. *Comprende?*"

"Yes, indeed. Well, thank you anyway. The room looks very comfortable."

"You mean okay?" His tone was offhand.

"Absolutely okay."

"*Bueno.*" He slammed the door cheerfully as he left.

She dropped her purse on the mirrored dressing table and then hovered uncertainly in the middle of the room. Normally, she would have made a beeline to the bed for the novelty of at last stretching out on a soft, immovable object.

This time, a glimpse in the mirror made her acknowledge that washing her face and applying new lipstick were at the top of the priority list. If Chris phoned to say that he wouldn't need her services for the rest of the night, she could always wash it off and head for bed.

As she ran the water in the basin and admired the tile counter, part of her mind was still reliving their newest encounter. She *would* have to be looking like a consumption victim in the last throes, she thought, scowling at her flushed cheeks and bedraggled hairdo. Especially when Chris was looking so fit. She'd forgotten how tanned he could become ... how well his clothes fitted him. But he must have lost weight in South America, she decided. There was a taut look on his face despite his casual surface air. As if he'd been working too hard ... too long ... or socializing too much.

A noisy gurgling made her look down to see water pouring out the overflow drain at the basin's rim. Hastily she shut off the taps and wiped off the drops which had spattered onto the tile counter. Another thirty seconds and she would have been mopping the floor as well. It was time to stop daydreaming.

She had just finished rinsing and drying her face when a knock sounded on her door. She went to open it, hoping that the maid who was probably coming to turn down the bed wouldn't attempt a long conversation. If she did, Amanda thought ruefully, it would turn out to be a monologue.

Opening the door, she realized that she needn't have worried. Chris had his knuckles poised to rap again and she almost received them on the bridge of her nose.

He rocked back on his heels, disconcerted. "I was about to give up. I thought you'd gone out." When she merely continued to stare at him, he added,

"Would you mind saying something? Preferably 'Come in.' I'd just as soon not hold a conference here in the hall."

Amanda stepped back and gestured him into the room. Then, realizing she was still clutching the towel, she gestured toward the chairs by the window. "Sit down over there while I comb my hair. I had the water running—that's why I didn't hear you knock."

Her logical explanation wiped the frown from his face. "Oh, I see." There was another awkward pause before he pulled a tacky bouquet of flowers from behind his coat and thrust it at her. "These are for you. They're the best I could find when I scouted round the neighborhood."

Amanda's heart took an unexpected lurch as she cradled the bunch of orange carnations mixed with tiger lilies. They were a far cry from the long-stemmed roses in Los Angeles but it was a nice gesture. Maybe Chris was regretting his recent behavior and this was his way of telling her. She looked up eagerly, only to hear him say, "I thought I owed you something after standing you up in Los Angeles."

"I see." To hide the bewilderment and hurt in her eyes, Amanda buried her nose in the blossoms but brought it up again promptly. Instead of the pungent spicy smell she expected, there was only one word to describe it. "Fish!" she said faintly. "They smell like fish."

"I know." Chris rubbed the back of his neck. "I meant to tell you. The fish market down the next block was the only place that had any flowers. They used them to decorate their showcase. To be honest, the fellow said they were about to throw them out."

She managed to smile. "It doesn't matter. They're very colorful. I'll put them in the basin until the maid can find a vase." She gestured again toward the chairs. "Sit down, won't you. This will just take a minute."

When she reentered the bedroom, he was sprawled in an armchair staring down at Avenida Juarez. Now that the troublesome bouquet had been presented, his expression was politely noncommittal. The same way he'd looked on the hotel steps.

Amanda wondered if it were going to be the guideline for his behavior, as well. He made a half-hearted attempt to rise as she came in and then sank back down as she perched on the edge of the bed.

"You're looking very well, Amanda. Your job must agree with you."

Amanda's eyes narrowed. From the way he spoke, he might have been discussing a required course with a freshman student. "It's fine, thanks. Did you have a good trip to South America?"

"Interesting," he said carefully. "I was able to do some research that I wanted."

"That's nice." Her eyes met his. "I loved your letters."

A wave of red surged under his tanned cheeks at her sweetly sarcastic tone and he eyed her warily. "They haven't worked out a zip code for the upper Amazon yet and they have a hell of a time getting mailmen for regular collections," he pointed out. "Besides, letters aren't a solution for anything. I didn't see any point in adding to the confusion in our case."

"So you gave me plenty of time to sort it out alone." She managed to keep her tone level. "Thanks a lot. The next time you ask a woman to marry you, you might explain your rules in advance."

An edge of anger sounded in his voice. "Or

present a blueprint for a Five-Year plan the way you wanted."

"I didn't suggest anything of the sort. Just because I didn't drop everything . . . oh, why are we rehashing it now? Even if we *did* do the sensible thing"—she paused for a second as if hoping he'd deny it and then went on hurriedly when he didn't—"there's no use raking over the remains. That's why I can't understand why you wanted me on this book. Things were bad enough when we were miles apart. But now—" She broke off again and bit her lip in annoyance. Every time she opened her mouth, she was in trouble. There was no point in advertising how awful those months had been.

Chris stirred uneasily on the chair, looking as if her confession embarrassed him. His next words confirmed it. "Actually I called you in for this because I needed a woman for window dressing in Yucatán. The book's practically finished. You can have the manuscript any time you want."

She ignored his last words. "What in the dickens do you mean . . . window dressing?"

"There isn't time to explain. I promised Constancia I'd meet her for cocktails in the lobby before she catches a plane to Yucatán and I'm late now." He stood up and made for the door. "You might as well join us when you get changed."

"Just a darned minute!" She caught up with him. "I'm not stirring an inch until you tell me what you're talking about. Who is Constancia?"

"A woman I know," he muttered. "She and her brother have a big hacienda down there. We'll be staying with them when we fly down tomorrow." He glanced at his watch and pulled open the door. "At least, we *will* be if I ever get down to the lobby. Come along when you're ready, but I'd better warn you in advance that Constancia's not very keen on threesomes. Something to do with her Latin temperament, I suppose." The last was said with a mocking grin before he disappeared into the hallway.

Amanda stared mutinously at the door which he'd closed behind him. Then she spent the next twenty minutes arraying herself in the most striking outfit she had in her suitcase. If the unknown Constancia planned to object to an extra woman, she might as well have a valid reason.

When she finally surveyed herself in the mirror, she decided that her efforts had definitely paid off. The dinner pajamas in splashy orange chiffon hugged her hips closely before belling seductively at her ankles. The bodice was a tribute to the designer's art, with a slashed neckline and full sleeves which narrowed to a tight cuff at the wrist. Her hair was pulled severely back to match the sophisticated image. She dabbed a discreet amount of French Lily perfume at her neckline and thought of Chris's bouquet which was now on the bureau. She really should add a little perfume to the water to camouflage the odor of cod and haddock.

While she waited for the elevator, she speculated whether he had given a similar bouquet to Constancia. And then as she stepped out in the lobby and saw them in an alcove by the doorway, she knew that her hopes were in vain. Even a quick look confirmed that Constancia was the orchid type. After a longer look, Amanda decided she might as well have worn a feedbag, for all the impression she would make.

Constancia was in her late twenties with a short figure which might become too voluptuous in later years but at the moment held only exciting curves. These were well displayed by a black taffeta dinner suit with crisp touches of white at the throat. Her lustrous black hair was drawn back in a French twist and her olive skin was enhanced by eye makeup and scarlet lipstick. Gleaming diamond earrings matched a brooch on her left shoulder and drew envious glances from every woman in the lounge, just as her profile acted like a magnet to every passing male.

Amanda moved across the marble floor as if she were headed for a session with the dentist's drill. Chris got to his feet as she approached and pulled out the extra chair beside them.

"I see you finally made it," he drawled. "I was about to have you paged. Constancia ... may I present Amanda Stewart. Amanda, this is Constancia Melgar."

Amanda's polite "How do you do" was interrupted by a spurt of laughter from the other woman.

"Honestly, Christopher." She put a subtle intimacy in her reproach. "What a way to introduce the poor girl. If I hadn't known she was your betrothed, I would have thought you didn't care at all." She reached across to pat his arm, as her dark-eyed glance challenged Amanda. "But aren't you clever not to let it bother you? Sit down and tell me how you captured this elusive man and why Christopher has kept you such a deep dark secret. I didn't know a thing about you until I met him in Los Angeles on this trip."

Amanda sank into the chair, mainly because her knees suddenly lost their stiffening. Chris was sitting down again with a rueful expression on his face. Was that because he was startled by Constancia's announcement as well?

Amanda opened her lips to explain the mistake when she received a warning kick under the table.

"Ouch! That's my foot," she protested.

"Darling ... I'm sorry. Did I hurt you?" Chris

leaned over to capture her hand, squeezing her fingers significantly as he did. "I didn't mean to beat you *before* we're married—blame it all on my big feet." He turned to Constancia with an easy grin. "And you needn't start criticizing my technique. No man makes love in a hotel lobby if he can take advantage of those garden walks at the Hacienda. I've told Amanda what a beautiful place you have."

Constancia smiled and leaned forward to pick up her cocktail glass. "Perhaps you should change your mind and make this a honeymoon trip instead of working all the time." She let her glance slide on to Amanda. "Why don't you try to persuade him? Miguel and I would be delighted. We can guarantee you all the privacy you want. Our season's almost over."

Chris's fingers gave another warning squeeze. Other than that, he looked just like an attentive fiancé, Amanda thought, and wondered if she'd missed the first chapter of the story. She forced herself to concentrate on his explanation.

"Remember, darling, I told you about Constancia and her brother running the Art and Handicraft Center at the Hacienda? They've turned it into one of the real showplaces of Yucatán."

"Oh, yes, of course." Amanda kept her tone soft but firmly moved her hand out of reach before the bruises began to show. "Seeing you again after all these months has driven every thought out of my head." She smiled and leaned back in her chair, deciding to do a little bloodletting herself. "Tell me more about the Hacienda, Constancia. Are you serious about offering it for a honeymoon?"

"Why, of course." The other woman looked startled but rallied quickly. "I'm not sure what the legal requirements for marriage are between two nonresidents, but Miguel could find out for you as soon as you arrive. Probably the American consul at Mérida could tell us. As a matter of fact, he's a good friend of our family."

Amanda turned back to Chris and noted his scowling face with satisfaction. "Maybe we could change our plans, then. What do you think, dear?"

He looked as if he could hardly keep his hands off her neck although his voice was carefully regretful. "God knows, I'd like to, angel. But there's a deadline on that manuscript." He turned to Constancia. "When I go on my honeymoon, I don't plan to surface for a good month or so. Since that isn't possible now, maybe we'd better take a raincheck on your offer."

"Whatever you say," she murmured.

"Oh, dear. I was afraid of that." Amanda made sure that her sigh sounded properly woebegone.

Chris heard it and swung back to regard her, his eyes narrowed. Obviously he'd tumbled to her bit of play-acting. "On the other hand," he drawled, "maybe we should live life as it comes and to hell with the manuscript. It's up to you, Amanda."

She gave him a withering look. "We can keep Constancia's offer in mind if the manuscript goes faster than we think . . ."

"Or the warm tropical nights make you too passionate to handle," he added. "I'm looking forward to that."

Constancia wasn't pleased by the turn the conversation had taken. She reached down at her side and picked up her purse. "I have to go or I'll miss my plane. I'm sorry you changed your reservations, Chris." She bestowed a smile on him before explaining to Amanda. "Originally the plan had been for all of us to go on to Yucatán tonight but Chris felt you might need a night here to get acclimated after your long flight." She stood up and lingered by her chair. "A good rest should have you looking better in no time. Probably it's all for the best." Then she stretched out her hand to Chris. "Come on, I insist that you see me to my taxi."

"I fully intended to." He paused to give Amanda a stern look. "I'll see you when I get back, so don't try any monkey business."

Amanda subsided in her chair, but when he reappeared a little later her chin was tilted at a rebellious angle. "You know, you needn't have bothered to change your plans for me. I could certainly have found my way to Yucatán alone. If I managed Mexico City after a detour via the Pacific coast, what's another side trip?"

"I knew I hadn't heard the end of that," he said, pulling her to her feet. "C'mon, if we're going to fight, let's do it during dinner. I'm starved."

She let him steer her toward the bank of elevators. "I'm merely stating a fact. What are we going this way for?"

"Because the restaurant is up on the twentieth floor. Any objections?"

"Certainly not. You just don't ever tell me anything. I'm surprised you don't write mystery novels—you have a natural talent for them."

There was a significant silence after that until the elevator operator let them out at the restaurant level. They stepped into a dimly lighted room with paneling on the walls and damask-covered tables. There was a good sprinkling of diners but the maître d' managed to find a place for them next to the long windows overlooking the park.

"Ummm," Amanda smiled as she examined the

magnificent view. "Just look at that illuminated fountain by the sidewalk! What a gorgeous sight."

"I thought you'd like it." Chris was concentrating on an outsized menu. "How does steak sound, or would you rather have something else?"

"Steak's fine—but I'll leave it to you."

He nodded and went into a huddle about their dinner with the dining room captain. When the order was taken and waiters were sent scurrying, Chris leaned back in his chair and surveyed Amanda. "Okay, now let's have some explanation. What kind of a game were you playing with Constancia?"

"Hah! If that isn't a typical masculine reaction—" She broke off as a waiter deposited a basket of rolls on the table but when he had disappeared, she went on again. "What was I supposed to say when a perfect stranger starts arranging my honeymoon. You're darned lucky I didn't call your bluff earlier." Her eyes were stormy as they met his across the table. "Exactly how long have we been engaged?"

"I thought women kept track of those things." He sounded unperturbed. "Simmer down, Amanda. There's no harm done, but next time make sure *you* follow the rules."

"There won't be a next time," she told him pointedly. "Anyone could see that Constancia wasn't serious about offering the Hacienda for a honeymoon. As it is, I'll be about as welcome as a can-can dancer at a bishops' convention."

"I fail to see the connection unless you have hidden talents—you're simply imagining things. What's wrong with Constancia?"

"If you can't tell by now, then you've been out of circulation too long." She picked up her spoon to start in on a melon ball cocktail, "I don't see why you need me as a 'fiancée' in the first place. Surely you're not trying to make her jealous?"

"What's wrong with that idea? It's worked before."

"Not with a woman like Constancia. She'd go after the competition with a sharp knife." Amanda tried to keep her voice dispassionate. "You didn't tell me that this job would be so hazardous. I should demand hardship pay."

"You don't know the half of it. There's another reason for wanting this extra night here."

Amanda felt inexpressibly cheered that the stopover wasn't for the therapeutic reason Constancia had indicated, but his next words made her joy shortlived.

"Not that you don't look as if you could use some sleep. What in the devil have you been doing in New York?"

"Working," she said briefly, not about to admit that his absence had anything to do with it. "Let's get on with the real reason for my being here. I gather you don't need my help on your manuscript?"

"Do what you want with that. Right now, I don't give a damn." He frowned as he waited for a still-sizzling tenderloin to be placed in front of him. "I haven't had any peace and quiet since Constancia suddenly appeared in Los Angeles this week ... all ready to be wined and dined."

He didn't sound like a man who was delighted by the interruption, Amanda thought. Maybe those lines of fatigue around his eyes meant that he had simply been working too hard.

"Well, in that case, why don't we just eat dinner now," she suggested with newfound wisdom. "Afterwards, we might go for a walk in the park and you can tell me what I need to know."

"I'd like that," he said simply, sounding like his

old self. "Eat your steak while it's hot. After that, we'll take things as they come."

The interlude that followed was like a blessed calm in the midst of a storm. Chris's face lost its strained look and Amanda felt herself relax as they enjoyed the delicious dinner.

Afterwards, Chris took her arm as they dodged through the traffic of Avenida Juarez before entering the confines of the park beyond. There were some strolling couples on the curving paths but not enough to dispel the quiet atmosphere provided by the trees and fountains.

They were amused to see that, despite the hour, the Mexican free-enterprise system was in full sway with pushcart vendors doing a brisk business. They passed a man selling corn on the cob and lingered to watch him spread it with mayonnaise, roll it in grated cheese, and finally douse it with hot sauce before handing it over to the purchaser. Nearby an old woman tended a smoky griddle to turn out pancakes which were thickly spread with jam when they were sold. Around a bend in the path, another woman sat on the grass with cherries and pine nuts piled on a cloth beside her.

"We needn't have bothered to eat at the hotel," Amanda said. "This is a real progressive dinner—appetizers to dessert."

Chris grinned. "Your stomach might object in the morning. I want you in good shape to get on the plane, so don't try any adventures in eating tonight."

"Well, I can enjoy the weather at least. I was afraid the rainy season would be in full swing by now."

"This month is the borderline. It'll be hot and muggy in Yucatán." He stopped in front of a stone bench, motioned for her to sit down and then settled restlessly beside her. "Look, Amanda, now that I've got you here, I'm not sure your coming was such a good idea. Maybe the best thing would be for you to take the next plane back to New York."

Amanda frowned at his profile, wondering what had happened to cause his indecision. Usually Chris's mind went down one track like the Metroliner. "Why don't you let me decide that," she said finally. "I gather it doesn't have anything to do with the book."

"Not directly. The book just gave me an excuse for coming back again. This problem began about five months ago when I was on my way to the Amazon." He ignored the slight stiffening of her figure as he continued tonelessly. "My plane had a few hours' stopover at Mérida so I decided to call a friend of mine who lives there. José took some of my classes a few years ago. He's an archaeologist who's a real nut on Mayan ruins."

"There's nothing strange about that, is there? After all, half the people in Yucatán are experts in Maya lore."

"Hear me out, will you?" He sounded annoyed.

"I'm sorry—"

His voice cut into her apologetic murmur as if she hadn't spoken. "I was surprised when José ... José Origa ... insisted in driving out to the airport to talk to me, but I hadn't seen him for a while and I supposed he wanted to hash over old times. I tried to dissuade him . . ."

"Why was that?"

"If you must know, I wasn't feeling sociable just then. Which was *your* fault." Before she could respond, he continued in a determined tone, "José insisted that he had something to tell me. He no sooner arrived at the airport than he dragged me off to a secluded corner and told me he had been doing some work in Quintana Roo ... that's a province on the south coast. He'd returned home for a few days because of his mother's illness but he'd just heard from his partner on the dig about a real treasure in the tomb they'd been excavating."

"I didn't know the Mayan finds had much intrinsic value. I thought the gold was generally a low-grade alloy and the rest of the stuff mainly ceramic or jade."

"You're right to a certain extent," Chris's tone was impatient. "At least that's what the last expedition found when they attempted to raise the treasures of the Sacred Well at Chichen Itza."

"I remember that. There were pieces of gold and stone sculpture but mostly they just brought up bones of women and infants." Amanda shuddered as she spoke. "And most everything was broken ... destroyed even before they threw it in the water. I'll never forget reading about the Bells of Death with their clappers smashed."

"Like the human sacrifices ... silenced forever," Chris agreed. "But don't forget ... it was the sacred well of sacrifice and the victims thought they would achieve everlasting life in the other world." He half-turned on the bench and raked his fingers through his hair. "How the hell did we get on the well at Chichen Itza? You're as bad at changing the subject as some of my freshmen."

"I was interested," she told him absently. "Besides, it's practically the only thing I know about Mayan treasures."

"Then belt up and listen. You might learn some more."

"I'm all ears ..."

Her quiet murmur brought a startled glance from

him. Suddenly he reached over to touch her pearl earring for a second before he shoved his hand back in his suit pocket. "Stop fishing for compliments. Now, where was I"

"Back in the airport at Mérida. Your friend, José, had just hit the jackpot," she said, staring determinedly at a man playing an old-fashioned barrel organ who was strolling by, and hoping she didn't sound as breathless as she felt.

"His partner had," Chris said, trying to ignore his momentary lapse. "But José was tremendously excited. They'd uncovered a golden disk about ten inches in diameter similar to the one found in the Sacred Well at Chichen Itza. Only there, the archaeologists only found one intact—the rest were in fragments. José said that his tomb appeared to contain at least a dozen perfect specimens. He was leaving that night to drive back to the site."

"I can see why he was excited." Amanda tried to concentrate. "It's funny I didn't read about it. Usually a find like that makes the papers. Was the tomb as rewarding as he hoped?"

"I don't know."

"You mean that he didn't write to you?"

"If he did, I didn't get the letter. Since I was traveling, I didn't think much about it at the time, but I was surprised not to find a letter waiting when I got back to Los Angeles. By then, I wanted to hear the end of the story. I wrote to his home in Mérida and last week received a reply from his brother who's an official in the Mexican government's Department of Antiquities. He said that José had disappeared that night. Apparently he told him the bare bones of the story—just as he had me—and started driving back to Quintana Roo. After that, there was no trace, and nothing to indicate that the treasure had ever been found. The authorities even put a special watch on flights leaving the area in case thieves tried to smuggle the disks out of the country."

"But what about José's partner? Couldn't he throw any light on the matter?"

"Nobody knew who the partner was; José hadn't confided his identity to anyone. Apparently he hadn't even told Constancia."

Amanda stared at him. "What does *she* have to do with it?"

"The dig wasn't far from their hacienda. José was staying with them when he unearthed the tomb."

"Well, didn't anybody notice who was with him during that time?"

"He was there for weeks. At one period or another, half the workers on the Hacienda were seen talking to him." Chris stretched his legs and surveyed his shoe-tops morosely. "Constancia told me that José's brother had interrogated the entire household staff without any luck. She and her brother, Miguel, had search parties out in the countryside for a solid week. But of course, there's no assurance that José ever left Mérida that night."

"I wonder why Constancia was so interested," Amanda said with sudden suspicion. "I can understand organizing search parties for a guest at the Hacienda but it seems a pretty flimsy excuse for calling on you in Los Angeles. *If* that's the excuse she used."

"There was nothing strange about it," Chris reproved. "Whatever impression she gave to you, Constancia has normal feminine feelings."

"From where I sit, I think she overdid the concern," Amanda insisted. "What did she think she could accomplish by seeing you?"

"At that point, she was desperate for any assistance she could get."

"But to call on a perfect stranger . . ."

"That's where you're wrong. I've known Constancia for quite a while. And it wasn't at all surprising that she enlisted my help," Chris stared back at Amanda with frank annoyance. "She was engaged to José. Most women take it pretty hard when they misplace a fiancé. Even temporarily."

"I see." Amanda tried to frame an apology but she couldn't find words. "That makes a difference," she managed finally. "And you say that she's never had the slightest word from him? Not one lead in all these months about where he could have gone—or what could have happened to him?"

"Not until a few days ago. Now things are all stirred up again."

Her eyes widened at the grim look which had settled over his face.

"Last week the police in Quintana Roo found the remains of a body in a shallow ditch near the Melgars' Hacienda. The authorities think it may be José." He met her gaze defiantly. "I'm going down there to find out."

Chapter Three

Amanda caught her first glimpse of the Yucatán peninsula as they came in for a landing at Mérida the next morning and thought that she had never seen such a desolate expanse of land in her life. Miles of unbroken greenery stretched beneath the plane as far as she could see. Even the long white sand beaches were without the slightest signs of human habitation. She mentioned it to Chris as the aircraft steward and stewardesses hastily stored breakfast trays and coffee pots before landing.

"Now I can see how a person could completely disappear in this country," she said soberly. "It's a wonder that they found any trace of José at all."

"We don't know they did. The last I heard, it was still an unidentified body. By now, I'm hoping that the authorities have decided one way or another." He reached over to check her seat belt. "There's no reason for this to spoil your trip. Yucatán's a fascinating place to visit. In the past most tourists came to see the ruins but now the coast is being developed like another Acapulco."

"You'd never know it from the way it looks around here," Amanda was staring out of the window beside her as the pilot banked for his approach. "I wasn't expecting another Mexico City but this looks like a map that's labeled 'Unexplored.'"

Chris put his hand comfortingly over hers as he saw her stiffen when the big plane swooped down for the landing. After the wheels had touched down, he removed it just as casually and peered past her shoulder as they taxied to the modern terminal. "It's not that bad. You know how they put airports out in the pastures. I hope they delivered the car I rented. It'll save time if we can pick it up here."

For a second, Amanda wondered if she should thank him for that moment of reassurance and then decided to ignore it as he had. Her gratitude spilled over into her smile though. "I take it that we're not spending long in Mérida?"

"Not this time." He was faintly apologetic. "I'd like to check with José's brother to see if there's any last-minute news. His office is downtown—close to the public market. You might enjoy wandering around while you're waiting."

Her smile widened as she released her seat belt and stood up. "You don't know what a chance you're taking. It might be safer to put me on a long leash."

"Not with this place." He waited until there was a break in the stream of people surging toward the exit by the cockpit and then motioned her to precede him. "There's nothing great about what they're selling—but you'll find plenty of atmosphere. Not like your neighborhood supermarket."

Later that forenoon, when Amanda was making her way back to where he'd parked the car, she felt Chris's description was a masterpiece of understatement. For one thing, her local supermarket was air-conditioned while the moisture-laden air around her felt as if it had been delivered from the nearest steam bath. She had unbuttoned the bodice of her green seersucker shirtwaist as far as the law and her conscience would allow but she was regretting her nylon stockings which were clinging uncomfortably. She paused under an awning to watch the other customers. The majority were barelegged and barefooted or, occasionally, wearing thongs or openwork sandals. All of them looked supremely comfortable; the men in their cotton pants and *guayaberras*—a thin overshirt with fine vertical tucks and pearl button decorations. The women had arranged their hair in cool braids and wore their *huipils*—a square-necked chemise outfit in white with a deep border of brightly colored embroidery at the neckline and hem. The dresses fitted loosely and were obviously designed for hot weather. Amanda could only stare enviously before looking down at her high-heeled pumps, wishing she could have two minutes alone with the shoe clerk who suggested them.

Unfortunately, the Mérida market didn't specialize in shoes but it had most everything else. She walked slowly on and surveyed the displays laid out on the broad cement sidewalk. If she'd been in the need of medical help, things would have been more promising. Headache remedies were popular and were sold in small plastic bags next to gruesome charts of the human body. One enterprising dealer had a dead snake coiled in a bottle of brine along with saucers of herbal remedies. Amanda's Spanish wasn't up to translating whether or not his prescriptions required an inch or two of snake carcass so she simply shuddered and walked on. The next display featured drug items with bottles of shampoo and hair spray piled haphazardly on the sidewalk alongside some religious pictures and nylon shopping bags.

She decided her favorite merchant was the man who sat by his display of cotton squares which were printed for embroidery. She chose two of them because they were so ridiculously cheap, although she couldn't translate the cross-stitch mottos. The needlework would give her something to do, she rationalized, and went on to purchase thread and other necessities by sign language.

Chris was waiting in the car for her, looking remarkably cool in a thin cotton shirt open at the throat. His suit coat and necktie had gone into the back seat as soon as they'd picked up the car at the airport.

"I didn't mean to keep you waiting," Amanda explained breathlessly, as she got into the car. "There were so many things to see and I wasted some time watching a man selling graters to mince vegetables . . ."

"A Mexican fast-pitch artist, eh? Relax. No harm done. I just got back myself." He grinned companionably. "What did you buy?"

She unwrapped the cotton squares self-consciously. "I couldn't resist these. They only cost a quarter—even without bargaining. The only trouble was that the man didn't speak English so he couldn't translate the mottos." She was spreading them on her lap as she spoke. "I hope it isn't 'Souvenir of the Cattle Show' or something like that."

Chris had trouble keeping a straight face. "Not exactly. One says 'Sleep well, my husband' and the other says 'I am always thinking of you, my heart.'"

"Oh, I see." Amanda could feel the color mounting in her cheeks as she searched for a safe reply. "Well, what do you know."

"You could put them in your hope chest," Chris suggested. "Unless hope chests went out when the women's movement came in. I doubt if Yucatán women have been hurrying to get on that bandwagon though."

Amanda was rolling up the offending cotton

squares. "It doesn't matter in the least. I can give these things away."

He looked skeptical. "Possibly. The one that says 'I'm always thinking of you, my heart' might do for an office Christmas party but 'Sleep well, my husband' is a little forthcoming unless you lead a swinging life in New York." He peered across at her. "I never thought to ask you about that."

Amanda slammed her purchases on the back seat with considerable force. She rolled down her side window and said pointedly, "I'm ready to go whenever you are."

Chris smothered a grin as he reached for the ignition switch. "We're on our way, then. Too bad this car doesn't have air-conditioning."

"At least the breeze helps." Amanda was willing to overlook his teasing now that they were underway. "Are we going right to the Hacienda?"

He nodded, concentrating on threading the car through pushcarts and pedestrians on the narrow street. It wasn't until later when the traffic had thinned at the edge of the business district that he elaborated. "More or less. We'll probably want to stop for something cold to drink on the way but I told Constancia that we'd get there some time this afternoon." He accelerated as the two-lane road cleared ahead of them and the last scattered buildings gave way to farmland.

Amanda half-turned to face him. "What did you find out when you spoke to José's brother? I gather you *did* see him."

"Yeah, there wasn't any trouble about that, but frankly I don't know whether it's good news or bad."

"What do you mean?"

"They've checked dental records and decided that

the body isn't José's. At least, his brother is sure of it."

"I should think you'd be delighted," Amanda began. "That means there is still a chance—"

He cut in impatiently. "Don't be infantile ... of course I'm glad, but I'm also realistic. Five months have gone by. Even José's brother acknowledges that the possibility of finding him alive is hellishly slim. The one positive sign is the fact that José's treasure hasn't hit the market and that treasure was the only logical reason for getting rid of José ... if his disappearance was deliberate."

"I can understand that. But how can you know what's happened to the treasure? There must be dozens of ways to get it out of the country."

"At least three or four," he acknowledged. "But it's hard to market the stuff afterwards. There isn't a reputable museum in the world that will buy artifacts without papers showing the country of origin. More important," he tapped a long finger on the steering wheel for emphasis, "they need a certificate of release from the government of that country okaying the export."

Amanda pursed her lips thoughtfully. "I see how that could eliminate the reputable markets, but it still leaves collectors who aren't particular about details."

"I don't dispute that. On the other hand, José was convinced his find was the greatest Mayan treasure yet. Golden disks still intact—covered with inscriptions that could give archaeologists new hope for deciphering the Mayan hieroglyphs." Chris's voice was laced with enthusiasm. "There isn't a price tag on a find like that, Amanda! If someone *did* get to it before José, he's not going to sell it for peanuts. When it does surface, the international Fine Arts Commission will hear about it."

She nodded and absently unzipped her purse in search of a handkerchief. The hot breeze coming in the car window was so laden with moisture that she was wishing she could ask Chris to stop and let her change into a pair of shorts. Since that wasn't possible, she dabbed at her forehead with the handkerchief and thought longingly of a cold shower.

"What in the devil do I smell?" Chris asked.

Amanda stiffened. "I don't smell anything. . ."

"There's something fishy," he insisted and then shook his head. "The heat must be getting to me. Imagine smelling fish in the middle of a sisal plantation."

"Is *that* what this is?" Amanda closed the zipper on her purse, trying not to show her anxiety. She'd forgotten about the carnation that she'd salvaged from her fish market bouquet and carefully pressed inside her address book before leaving Mexico City. "I didn't know they grew sisal here," she said brightly.

Chris's look indicated that he'd thought better of her. "Where do you think rope comes from?"

Amanda could have told him that she wasn't concerned about what grew along the roadside. Instead, she was wondering how long he was going to adhere to his irritating brotherly manner. Ever since he'd taken her back to her hotel room in Mexico City, he'd kept a pleasant but impersonal distance between them. If he'd ever been befuddled enough to think he was in love with her, he'd promptly dropped the idea while he was away and probably uttered thanks each night for his provident escape. This time he'd emphasized that their "engagement" was strictly for appearance's sake. Nothing more.

It wasn't that she cared, Amanda told herself, but it would be nice if he stopped treating her like a dim-witted relative who'd been wished on him for the holidays!

"Now what's wrong?" Chris observed her frowning profile and answered his own question. "Heat exhaustion probably. You should have stayed out of the sun at the market. Or had enough sense to wear a hat . . ." He braked and pulled the car over to the shoulder of the road.

Amanda looked around in confusion. "Why are you stopping here?"

He turned off the ignition and reached over the back of the seat. "You haven't heard a word I've said. It's a good thing I put in something cool to drink—you'll feel better after you get some liquid down." He was fumbling in his camera case for a bottle opener and muttered with satisfaction when he found it.

"Really, Chris—there's nothing wrong with me . . ."

"That's what you think," he said in kindly fashion, handing her the cold bottle of pop. "You aren't the type to go off into brown studies. If it isn't the heat—it's probably jet fatigue. Maybe you'd feel better if you got in the back seat and put your feet up . . ."

"Oh, for heaven's sake!" Her angry outburst fizzled as she recognized his concern. "Honestly, I'm fine. Or at least as fine as anybody could be in this temperature. It feels like a New York subway in August."

"I know." He grinned as he opened his own bottle of pop before slouching back in the seat. "But there is one difference—this air doesn't smell like salami."

Amanda nodded and rubbed the iced cola bottle

against her flushed cheek. After an uneasy period of silence, she said, "So that's sisal. It looks like a great overgrown cactus garden, doesn't it?" Her eyes roamed the endless rows of three- and four-foot high plants whose swordlike leaves reached toward the sun. "I'd hate to try a parachute jump into the middle of it."

"Around here, nobody would pay any attention if you did. Sisal, or *henequen* as they call it, thrives on neglect. The plants prefer a long growing season and a rocky, arid soil."

"Which makes it a natural for this part of the country," Amanda decided after another glance at the bleak countryside. "How do they get it from that"— she nodded toward the green plants—"to packages of twine in a hardware store? In sentences of twenty-five words or less," she added.

"I'm surprised you don't want the Theory of Relativity explained on the head of a pin."

"That can be your encore," she said. "I take it that they cut the leaves . . ."

"Eight to twelve of them each time they harvest."

"Which is?"

"Every three months. Is that brief enough?" Then he relented. "They used to ship the stuff from a Yucatán port called Sisal—that's how the plants got their name. Now most of it's exported from Progreso."

Amanda nodded as she stared at a big plant close to the car. "I suppose they have to get the fibers out some way . . ."

"Go to the head of the class," Chris said. "These days it only takes about five seconds to run a leaf through a machine. When it comes out at the other end, it's kind of a fibrous spaghetti. Nothing's thrown away or wasted in the process; they're even starting to get tequila from *henequen*."

She wrinkled her nose at him. "Now I understand why you're such an authority."

He grinned and put his empty pop bottle on the floor as he started the car. Then he glanced over his shoulder before pulling back onto the road. "These days, the sisal market is booming again since synthetics are getting so expensive. That's one reason for the happy faces on the farmers around here. They're back in the money again."

"It's funny how everything seems to go full circle eventually. At first, I thought it was only women's hemlines . . ."

"Or men's collar styles." He looked amused. "I wonder when my celluloid ones will come back in style?"

"Any day now, I suppose." She was staring at the deserted highway ahead of them. "So if the sisal market is back in the money, the economy around here gets a shot in the arm. Right?"

"In twenty-five words or less," he teased. "You bet! Constancia was mentioning it in Mexico City. Said it was like a miracle after the lean years."

"She didn't give the impression that she was worrying about her next welfare check. That outfit she was wearing didn't come from Filene's basement—unless Givenchy and Halston have set up a boutique down there."

Chris raised an eyebrow. "Don't most women want to look as attractive as possible?"

"Of course they do." Amanda's cheeks flushed even redder, making her feel like a stoker on a boiler gang. "I just meant that Constancia didn't look as if she were down to her last meal."

"You're right about that. When her family's sisal plantation began losing money, she and her brother started a handicraft center for their workers and opened the Hacienda to visitors. Now they have more orders than they can handle for their ceramic stuff and a waiting list of guests for the Hacienda." He let the car's speed slacken as they approached a small village which consisted mainly of a few huts facing the road and a shack where they sold bottled pop. They went by a small boy who had his arms full of empty bottles but managed to grin at the car.

"I don't think I've seen an unhappy face since we left Mérida," Amanda mused as they passed the last of the huts and saw two village women giggling while they filled their plastic buckets from a communal water faucet. "Darned if I can see how they can manage to laugh. Imagine carrying all your water and living in a one-room hut! And the huts are just made of sticks, aren't they?"

"Sticks held vertically in dried mud with a roof of palm thatch."

"Plus a hard dirt floor." Amanda made a grimace of distaste. "The only furniture I could see was a hammock."

"There's nothing wrong with hammocks. They're cooler than beds because the air can circulate underneath them. And when they're not in use, you hang them on a hook at the end of the room. That way, there's no waste space. You'll find hammocks all over Yucatán—even in expensive homes in Mérida. Of course, a hammock *does* have certain drawbacks——"

"I can imagine," she cut in before he could go on. "Anyhow, I think these people are wonderful. Most of us would shudder if we had to live in such primitive conditions."

His expression sobered. "You're right about that. Maybe that's why Constancia and Miguel had such luck getting skilled labor for the Handicraft Center.

The living conditions at the Hacienda are a damned sight better than the average village life."

Amanda let her head rest back against the seat. "I'm glad to hear that. The prospect of bathing in a plastic bucket wasn't appealing."

"That's the trouble with civilized women."

"If I remember, *you* were the one ordering steak for dinner last night," she pointed out. "You've strayed quite a ways from the 'back to nature kick' yourself."

"With good reason. You should have been with me on the Amazon . . ." he began and then stopped in mid-sentence. "Maybe it's safer if we forget about that."

Especially since I wasn't invited, Amanda thought grimly, staring out her side of the car. "The scenery isn't the greatest, is it?" she said at last when it appeared that he wasn't going to break the silence. "Just flat land with scrub trees and underbrush between sisal plantations. I thought it would be more of a jungle."

He looked amused. "We've barely scratched the surface of the country. Wait until we drive into Quintana Roo later on. It's a great game province—wild turkey, deer—even jaguar. Nobody has trouble getting fresh meat for the table."

Amanda's eyes widened. "Jaguar . . . right out in the countryside! That sounds more like Africa than Mexico."

"Not to anybody who knows Yucatán. That's one theory for José's disappearance. If he traveled alone into that area, any number of things could have happened."

"You mean you know where he was excavating?" Amanda sat up straight again, her anger forgotten.

"I can make an educated guess. But don't get any

hopes up—more than one person has the same idea. Don't forget, archaeologists have been working around that area for years. Constancia said all of the old finds have been thoroughly ransacked by now. There's nothing of value left in any of the tombs."

Amanda stared at his tight jawline. "But you have another idea, haven't you?"

"I promised Constancia I'd take a look around," he said, choosing his words with care. "She thought that since I was one of the last people to talk to José I might find something in the area that the rest of them had overlooked. Since my publishers couldn't wait to get me working with my editor," his voice deepened with amusement, "I decided I might as well . . ."

". . . take care of a whole flock of birds while you were about it." Her lips settled in an ominous line. "And you accuse women of being devious!"

"Not I. I never generalize—each woman should be considered on her own merits. Now you, for example. Who would think that such a pocket-sized female could be so stubborn and hard-headed . . . or need so much sleep." The latter comment was added as he saw her trying to stifle a yawn. "I'll assume it isn't the company you're keeping."

"That's big of you." She yawned again, making no attempt to hide it this time. "Do you mind analyzing me another afternoon? I can't keep my eyes open. It must be the heat," she added reluctantly.

"Go ahead and take a nap. There's another remedy but I'd better not try it when I'm driving."

"I should think not." Amanda tried to sound properly indignant but it was hard when her eyelids were drooping. "Be sure and wake me up if anything interesting happens." She shifted slightly and propped her body against the side of the car.

Chris reached out to pull her toward him. "There's no use bouncing your head against that glass. Relax, girl"—this when she stiffened and started to move away. "Take advantage of a shoulder when it's offered. No strings attached."

Amanda wavered and then settled back against him with a soft sigh. It was where she'd wanted to be from the beginning, she realized. At least now she had an excuse and she'd be a fool not to make the most of it. She was still smiling about that when her eyelids went down again and stayed down for the count.

It was a detour onto a short section of graveled road which eventually roused her. She awakened slowly, blinking in confusion as she realized that her nose and cheek were snuggled tightly against a masculine chest and that she was being held by the masculine arm which apparently went with it. Then full consciousness returned and she sat up so fast that her head swam. "For heaven's sake, why didn't you say something," she murmured to Chris. "You must be numb all along one side."

"I wasn't suffering," he said mildly. As she felt the tousled state of her hair and started to search for a mirror, he added, "You look all right—stop fussing."

"All right?" she echoed. A quick glance in her compact made her shake her head despairingly. "I look awful. Why didn't you wake me?"

"You needed the sleep," he replied. "And you'd have ended up with a crick in the neck if I hadn't held onto you. It was as simple as that."

"I'm terribly sorry," she began again.

"I don't know why. You were more interesting than the rest of the scenery. Incidentally, we're in Quintana Roo now—the Hacienda is only about a half hour away."

"But you've missed lunch . . ."

"If you'd seen some of the roadside stands, you'd realize that was a blessing in disguise. Besides, I thought you needed sleep more than food."

"Oh, I don't mind a bit," she said truthfully, feeling better after using a moist towelette on her forehead and wrists. "I'd offer you one," she told Chris, "but I guess you wouldn't want to smell like jasmine. I could take a turn at the wheel, though."

"I'll make you do double duty on the return trip. Damn! Why don't they fix those potholes?" He frowned as he saw her rubbing an elbow. "Are you hurt?"

"Not really." She was looking curiously out at the flat landscape which had changed from arid farmland to scrub forest and palmetto thicket during her nap. "That undergrowth looks dense. I'd hate to have to get through it on foot."

"This is the wild game country I was telling you about. I've passed half a dozen farmers on bicycles with rifles slung over their shoulders."

"Then I'm just as glad I was asleep." She fell silent as she saw a figure flagging them down beside a stopped car. "Now what!"

Chris hit the brake slowly, taking care not to fishtail the car in the loose gravel. "Damned if I know. That isn't any native."

"Not unless he buys his clothes from Bill Blass." Amanda was staring at the man by the roadside. He was tall and well dressed in bone-colored slacks and a beige herringbone jacket. "He looks as if he's a refugee from Palm Beach instead of Yucatán." She turned back to Chris. "Sure you didn't take a detour while I was asleep?"

He merely grinned and pulled up behind the other car, waiting until the dust had settled before rolling down his window. "Need some help?" he asked the man.

"Thank god, another American!" the other said with relief. "I thought I was going to have to bum a ride on the handlebars of the next bike that went past and that would have posed some problems." He stuck out a hand. "My name's Kent Ives . . . I'm from Miami."

"Chris Jarrow. This is Amanda Stewart."

"Miss Stewart." Ives ducked down to nod at her and shook hands with Chris. "I sure appreciate your stopping." He grinned. "That's putting it mildly. I would've welcomed a strolling porcupine at this point."

Despite his comment, it wasn't apparent that he was feeling any physical discomfort from being stranded by the hot roadside. He had shed his tie but that was his only concession to the temperature; his shirt was still immaculate and his jacket fit without a wrinkle. He looked to be in his late thirties and his assured manner tended to confirm it. Dark-rimmed glasses and a beak nose gave him an owl-like aura but his eyes gleamed with laughter under a thatch of hair so dark that it was blue-black in the sunlight.

"What happened . . . did your engine overheat?" Chris asked him.

"Hell, no! I ruined my right front tire—hit a rock on the shoulder of the road when I had to swerve. I never thought to check the spare when I picked up the car in Mérida. . . ."

"Flat?" Chris asked sympathetically.

"Nonexistent. Wouldn't you think I'd have known better! Can I hitch a ride with you to the closest telephone?"

"Sure—no problem," Chris said. "We're on our way to the Hacienda Melgar. You can take care of your business there. . ." His voice trailed off at the change in the other's face. "Did I say the right thing?"

"Did you ever! That's where I was heading for in the first place."

"Then we might as well move your stuff and be on the way. Somebody can come back with a spare tire and deliver your car to the Hacienda. Okay?"

"You bet!" An expression of unease suddenly passed over Ives's amiable features and he reached up to scratch his jaw with his thumb. "The only thing is—I've got a lot of gear."

"I noticed your fishing stuff," Chris jerked his head toward the other's back window. "Planning to try for some of the big ones before you go home?"

"Yeah, I thought I'd sneak in a few days at Cozumel or Isla de las Mujeres," Ives replied, naming the two islands off the coast which attracted scuba enthusiasts and sports fishermen from all over.

"We have plenty of room," Chris reassured him. "Amanda won't mind if I move her parcels back to the trunk."

"Of course not—or they can be shoved in my tote bag."

Chris nodded and opened the rear door. "That'll leave the back seat free for your gear," he told Ives. "Might as well bring it over."

"Okay. There's another thing, though . . ." Kent blurted out. "I've picked up an extra body. Oh, not literally," he added hastily as he saw their faces. "At least, it's not a dead body . . ."

"I'm glad of that," Amanda murmured.

"Maybe you'd better explain," Chris said warily.

Kent started to grin. "It's okay—I'm not a fugitive from the nearest nut factory. I told you I got the flat when I had to swerve onto the shoulder but I didn't say that the whole thing happened when this lame-brained dog came out of the underbrush to chase a bird across the road. Of course, I was driving too fast," he added ruefully. "I'll admit that—but you can see for yourself that there isn't any traffic on this road."

Chris cut into his rationalizing. "You mean that you've got an injured dog around here someplace?"

"That's it, exactly."

"Well, for heaven's sake . . . Where is he?" Amanda was opening her door. "The poor thing could die while we sit here discussing him."

"Hardly. He got a sore paw out of it, that's all." Ives had recovered his composure as he led them to his car. "The damnable part is he crawled up on the back seat and he's not about to leave. I don't know what to do." He gestured toward the dusty interior of his car. "Meet Junior."

Junior was one of the sorriest examples of dogdom on public view anywhere. He was black and unaccountably large, with a rugged mastiff's head looking strange on a thin hound's body. His wiry coat showed that his ancestry had been extensive if not selective. Just then he was stretched at full length on the upholstery licking a big bruised paw. He looked up to see three curious faces staring at him, and his tail came to life, raising a cloud of dust and beating a hollow tattoo against the fishing rods on the end of the seat.

"He's real good-natured until you try to haul him out of there," Kent said morosely. "And his teeth are just as big as the rest of him, so I didn't insist."

Amanda frowned as she surveyed the dog, who had gone back to nursing his paw. "He must be starving. I don't think he's eaten for days," she told Ives accusingly.

"Well, don't blame me. He wouldn't have caught that bird he was after—even if I hadn't clipped him. He was a good four feet behind."

"One thing, for sure, we can't leave him here," Chris said as the dog started to pant, his bony sides heaving with the effort. "We'll take him along to the Hacienda and sort it out there."

"Fine with me," the other man assured him, "but you tell him. We're suffering from a communications gap."

Chris cast a swift look down the deserted road. "Amanda, bring our car up alongside this one. Maybe we can convince Junior to change residence when he sees we're joining forces."

She smiled and hurried to do as he asked. In a very few minutes, Kent's luggage and fishing rods were transferred to the other car. Junior's big ears went up questioningly as the last piece went out, but other than pushing himself up to a sitting position and carefully elevating his left paw, he made no attempt to move.

"The poor thing! Look at him—he doesn't know what to do," Amanda said, when both Chris and Kent had whistled and snapped their fingers to no avail. Junior had obviously found the most comfortable niche he'd ever occupied in his precarious life, and, confused as he was, he didn't intend to leave it. He simply remained pressed against the seat despite all their urging.

"There's nothing else left to try—we'll just have to hoist him out," Chris said finally when he'd searched fruitlessly for some kind of leash and discovered the best they had was Amanda's embroidery thread. "I'll take his front end; you take the rear," he instructed Kent.

The other frowned. "I understand—but are you

sure Junior does? He might not take kindly to it and I'd hate to have you arrive at the Hacienda carrying your head under your arm."

"I'm not keen on it myself but I can't figure out any other way." Chris sounded at the end of his leash even if Junior wasn't.

"Let me have one last try," Amanda suggested. "Come on, Junior. Come on, boy." She reached out and scratched the matted hair behind his ears.

Junior cowered in confusion; in the past any attention directed his way had not been accompanied by honeyed words. Finally he relented enough to sniff her hand. Then, emboldened, directed his nose to her leather purse which was hanging over her arm.

"Looks as if he thinks that's a lunch bag," Kent joked. "Too bad you aren't carrying a ham sandwich in it."

"If Amanda had a ham sandwich in there, I'd be fighting Junior for it," Chris informed them. "Come on, there's nothing for it but to ... hey, look at that—he's moving! Take it slow, Amanda—"

"Uh-huh. Come on, baby," Amanda had unzipped her purse and held it suspended before Junior's nose like a carrot in front of a donkey. The dog's interest in her handbag had made her suddenly remember the fishy souvenir carnation she was still carrying. It might not be much of a love talisman but it was serving one useful purpose. Junior was following his quest with the zeal of a Crusader looking for an Infidel.

He clambered stiffly down from Kent Ives's car and limped over to the other vehicle, springing onto that back seat without a backward glance.

"Good boy, Junior!" Amanda zipped up her purse and put it safely beyond reach before patting his head.

Chris was still frowning. "I'll be damned if I can figure out what you did, but it certainly worked!" He shook his head dazedly and then took her by the elbow. "Get in the front seat. Junior needs a flea bath before he's acceptable company."

"I wonder how they're going to like our arriving with livestock in tow," Kent said, squeezing in beside Amanda and slamming the door. "I've never been to the Hacienda Melgar before but it sounds pretty posh."

"Well, they can't expect us to leave Junior bleeding on the road," Amanda said indignantly.

Chris gave the object in question a glance in the rear-vision mirror before putting the car in gear and starting off. "Don't worry, Constancia will understand once we explain. I just wish Junior wasn't quite so big." After another glance in the rear mirror, he added, "He seems to have recovered his appetite, Kent. He's sniffing at that cork handle on your rod."

"Cut that out, you lummox—" Ives commanded with a hasty glance over his shoulder. "Well, what do you know . . ."

Amanda was trying to squirm in the seat so she could look, too. "What now?"

"He stopped." Ives sounded like a proud father. "I'll be damned—I didn't think he understood English."

Chris broke out laughing. "Junior has discovered the advantage of being bilingual."

Amanda considered the big dog thoughtfully. "For his sake, it might be better if he doesn't understand Spanish when we get to the Hacienda."

"What do you mean by that?" Chris asked.

"Merely that it's a good thing you carry extra weight with Constancia——"

"Who is this Constancia?" Kent interrupted.

"She and her brother own the Hacienda," Chris told him briefly before switching his attention back to Amanda. "I don't know where you got that opinion of her. You really shouldn't make snap judgments of people, Amanda."

"Blame it on woman's intuition. Constancia's first impulse will be to throw Junior to the wolves—figuratively speaking, of course."

"I think you deserve to lose some money," Chris snapped. "Five will get you ten she won't do anything of the kind."

"Remember, I said *first* impulse—"

"There's nothing wrong with my hearing." He gave her a lordly masculine look. "You heard the bet. Kent, do you want to keep the stakes?"

"Sure, glad to." Kent shifted on the seat and let his arm rest along the top. "But if our landlady decides to toss Junior and me out into the cold, I hope you'll ask her to wait until after dinner."

"Oh, she won't toss *you* out." Amanda's meaning was perfectly clear.

Chris took his attention from the road. "I'm doubling the stakes," he informed her. "Your feminine intuition is off by a mile."

"That may be," she replied just as coldly, "but I'll wait and see."

Kent Ives glanced from one to the other with an amused expression. Then he looked over his shoulder to advise Junior conversationally, "Don't open your mouth, boy. The stakes are getting too high for us."

Chapter Four

As it happened, Amanda was close to losing her money.

When they drove into the Hacienda Melgar a few minutes later, she was so enchanted with its impressive Spanish architecture and luxuriant tropical gardens that she almost forgot about anything else.

The main building was a rambling two-story structure with a tile roof which was almost hidden by the trees and tropical plantings on the entrance drive. The poinciana or flame trees were in full bloom and their vibrant orange coloring drew attention like a magnet. Beds of philodendrons and hibiscus provided ground cover between them while purple, pink, and white bougainvillea hugged the stucco walls of the Hacienda. A fountain splashed gently in a shaded entranceway with mosaic tile floors, and a wrought-iron grill just beyond opened wide to reveal steps leading to the inner parts of the building.

Two men in spotless white uniforms appeared from the shaded interior as soon as Chris turned off the ignition. They had just gotten to the trunk of the car and Junior was still safely confined to the back seat when Kent cleared his throat. Amanda looked up to see Constancia advancing regally through the doorway.

Her eyes widened in sheer admiration as the Mexican woman glided down the steps wearing a flowing white gown that looked like a monk's habit except that Franciscans seldom wore pure white silk girdled with golden cord. An attached cowl was draped over her severely dressed hair giving her the aspect of a sophisticated Raphael madonna. Her final touch was pure spectacle: balanced on her outthrust wrist was a gorgeous parrot whose feathers were bright red, green, and blue.

Kent leaned across to Amanda's ear as she got out of the car, "If she's for sale, I'll buy two and don't bother with my change."

Amanda squelched him with a sideways glance and noted that Chris hadn't missed their exchange; he was keeping a straight face but his eyes sparked with laughter.

The Vision floated nearer and then stopped in surprise when she decided that Kent was a guest, too. Chris performed the necessary introductions.

"Constancia—this is Kent Ives. He was having car trouble when we found him down the road a bit." He turned to complete the introduction. "Senorita Melgar who owns the Hacienda."

"Mr. Ives, how nice!" Constancia was unexpectedly effusive. "I was beginning to wonder what had happened to you. I'm so sorry you had problems with your car."

"It was nothing serious," Kent replied. "I was lucky when Chris and Amanda happened along."

"Well, do come in," Constancia pressed hospitably. "Pablo ..." she signaled to the gray-haired man unloading their bags from the trunk. "Take care of their luggage—*inmediatamente.*"

"*Si, senorita ... de seguro.*"

"I have some fishing gear in the back seat and I

wanted to ask permission about another guest," Kent went on. "Hey—wait a second!"

Pablo, in his eagerness to unload the car, had opened the rear door. Like a genie from a bottle, Junior spurted from the interior with his tail thrashing. After a glance around, his eyes lit on the most colorful object and he bounded toward the parrot on Constancia's wrist. The bird uttered a shrill squawk of alarm and in a flurry of dusty feathers managed to wing his way to a palm frond overhead. Junior's deep bark of frustration mingled with Constancia's cry of rage as she tried to brush parrot feathers from her gown and resist the dog's enthusiastic advances at the same time.

"Pablo! *Aquel perro . . .*" Words failed her and she could only level a shaking finger at the black dog who, by then, had gathered his presence was something less than welcome. His tail crept between his legs and he cowered uncertainly.

Pablo hastily dropped an armful of fishing rods and advanced toward him.

His action triggered an immediate response from the others who had been stunned by the furor.

"Wait a minute!" Chris moved forward and stationed himself by the quivering Junior. "This dog's been hurt," he told Constancia.

"You can't mean that he belongs to you?" Her voice climbed.

"Well—yes."

"No—he's mine!" Kent said. He seemed a little taken aback by his indignant outburst but went on firmly. "I realize that I should have asked if you permitted dogs here, but I didn't have a chance."

Amanda plunged in. "You see, Junior's paw was injured and he didn't want to leave him with a vet. He would have been so lonesome."

Constancia's hands were tugging her robe back in place but her attention obviously was elsewhere. "Let me get this straight," she said softly. Her eyes were taking in Kent's immaculate sports coat and slacks. "You mean that . . . creature"—a scarlet-tipped finger leveled toward Junior—"that creature belongs to you?"

"Actually, we all have shares in him," Chris said firmly. "Normally he isn't so dirty but he tangled with some traffic on the road and came off second best when we were on the way here. I told Kent that you'd have someone who could care for him until we can ship him back to the States."

Constancia took another look at his determined face and capitulated. "Of course—I was just so startled, you understand. Pablo . . ."

The old man smiled. "Of course, *senorita*." He had reached in his pocket and found some twine which he fashioned into a rough leash for the subdued dog. "I will brush him and then find him something to eat," he said in fluent but accented English. He must have known that Junior's sponsorship was recent but his expression was kind as he leaned over the dog. After fondling the rough ears, he tugged on the leash.

Junior resisted long enough to give them a soulful look before padding around the corner of the building at the old man's side.

At least one individual was happy to see him go. The brilliantly colored parrot uttered a croak of triumph as he stared down at them.

"What a beautiful bird," Amanda muttered, mostly for something to say.

Constancia nodded. "That's Guaca . . . he's been here since my father's time. I suppose he'll spend the rest of the afternoon sulking." She shrugged. "It doesn't matter. Pablo can coax him into his cage later with some food. I imagine you'd like to see your rooms by now. If you're not used to our heat, it can be overpowering." She motioned for them to follow her with a graceful gesture.

Amanda skirted the palm, giving Guaca a wide berth.

Chris fell into step beside her, a few feet behind Constancia and Kent. "I'd say the whole thing was a draw, wouldn't you?"

She stopped beside the fountain. "I beg your pardon?"

"The bet. Come on, let's go. I keep thinking of the swimming pool and a long cold drink."

Amanda allowed herself to be led. "I'd forgotten about our bet. You'll admit that you-know-who"—she lowered her voice as she nodded to Constancia's figure ahead of them—"wasn't overjoyed by you-know-what."

"No, but she let him stay."

"Only after you and Kent stuck up for him."

"Uh-huh. But I have the feeling that Kent's defense was the important thing. S'funny—he didn't let on that he'd ever heard of her before. And now look at them."

Amanda frowned as she stared at the companionably close figures ahead of them. She turned to glance at Chris's profile and noted that he was merely looking thoughtful . . . not annoyed. "Well, Kent's a pretty tasty morsel," she said lightly. "He's nice, too."

Chris's fingers nipped her elbow. "Don't go getting ideas. He's too old for you."

"That's ridiculous. These days nobody pays any attention to a fifteen-year difference in age. You're simply out of touch with things." Even as Amanda argued she was wondering why she persisted in proclaiming her views. Kent obviously had made up his own mind.

Chris noticed it, too. "There's no use bothering over something that's an academic question . . ."

"I merely said that——"

"I know what you said," he cut in. "I'm telling you to stay in your own league and not go looking for side benefits on this job. Don't forget, you're down here to work. For me," he added with unnecessary emphasis. "There won't be time to indulge in extracurricular affairs."

"I'll try to remember." Her voice was carefully level. "Is it all right if we have the rest of the lecture after dinner? I'd like to look around on my own while you're registering . . . if you don't mind."

"And if I do?"

"There's really not much you can do about it." Amanda deliberately turned on her heel, aware that there was a great deal he could do about such insolence but relying on normal masculine inclination to avoid repercussions in public.

A moment later, she heard his footsteps receding on the tiled hallway and uttered a sigh of relief. At the same time, she wondered why Chris was so short-tempered. When they'd worked on his first book, they'd hardly exchanged a cross word. Of course then, he'd been falling in love with her; now he was viewing things more realistically.

She made an effort to concentrate on the beautifully proportioned stairway which led up to the guest wing. The shallow risers were of tile mosaic while the treads themselves were fashioned from beige Spanish marble. At the stair landing, a stained-glass window set in a wrought-iron frame reflected a rainbow of color against the whitewashed walls.

Amanda climbed the stairs slowly enjoying the framed displays of ancient Yucatán dress mounted on the wall, marveling at the fine embroidery and vibrant colors that had lasted over the years.

At the balcony level, the guest wing overlooked a lush garden area with a luxurious kidney-shaped swimming pool in the middle of it. Black-and-white tile mosaic was used for the pool surround and the curving walks leading to it.

Amanda's lips formed a soundless whistle of admiration. From this view, the Hacienda Melgar seemed more like an annex of Beverly Hills than a Yucatán guest house.

There was the soft padding of feet behind her and Amanda looked around to find the elderly Pablo bringing her bags up the stairs.

"Mees Stewart?" He smiled and the lines in his brown face deepened. "I have your key ... if you'll follow, please."

"Of course. How is Junior? Did he settle down?" She was hurrying to keep up with him as they moved along the columned porch which was furnished with rattan lounges at comfortable intervals.

Pablo slowed his steps to say, "Junior?" He gave the first letter a Spanish pronunciation as he explored the name. Then he grinned. "That one is a smart dog. They're feeding him in the kitchen now. Afterwards—I get him clean. When he knows me better." He put her bags down outside a door with screened louvers on its upper half and inserted a key. "This is your room, Miss Stewart." He gestured down the porch. "Senor Jarrow, he's next, Senor Ives at the end." Then, picking up her bags again, he led her into the room.

It was shaded and spacious with a ceiling fan whose blades started to circulate as soon as Pablo turned a switch by the door. Louvers on the far wall of the room covered a screened window which faced onto another garden area. As Amanda went over to look down, she felt as if she were perched in the top of the palm trees outside the window. Evidently a covey of birds clustered in the fronds felt the same way; they fluttered off with noisy chattering, clearly loath to welcome a new neighbor.

"The bathroom is here, *senorita*." Pablo opened an adjoining door and gestured toward an old-fashioned bath decorated in gleaming white tile from floor to ceiling.

"Everything looks very comfortable." Amanda dropped her purse onto a low table by the window and ran a hand through her hair. "What time is dinner served?"

"Not until seven thirty, Miss Stewart." Pablo lifted her luggage onto two leather-covered racks and paused by the door. "Senorita Melgar hopes you'll join her and the others for cocktails by the pool whenever you like."

"Is the pool open for swimming now?" Amanda asked, unsure whether she was supposed to show up in a bikini or an evening dress. For an instant, she regretted that she hadn't trailed Chris to the registration desk to find out the lay of the land.

Fortunately, Pablo was able to oblige. "I heard the gentlemen say they planned to swim before dressing for dinner. Senorita Melgar always goes in the pool about this time as well."

"Then I'll probably join them. Just a minute, Pablo," she caught him halfway through the door and put some folded peso notes in his palm. "If Junior needs a place to sleep later on, I'll be glad to share my room with him."

"Don't worry, *senorita*." White teeth gleamed against his leathery skin. "The gentlemen offered, too. After the dog is washed, then we see, eh?"

She smiled in response. "Fair enough. We'll let Junior pick his roommate." Then as he still lingered. "Is something wrong?"

"It might be better to ... not talk about this to Senorita Melgar. There is no need to bother her."

"Let sleeping dogs lie? Is that what you mean?"

His English was good enough to catch the quotation. "Exactly, *senorita*." He nodded and went out, closing the door behind him.

Amanda smiled as she kicked off her shoes and headed for the bathroom to wash her face. Pablo had evidently worked for Constancia long enough to know how to handle his fiery employer.

It didn't take her long to change out of her dress into a two-piece batik swimsuit. "It's easy to see that you should have been spending your weekends under a sun lamp, my girl," she told her reflection as she stared into a wall mirror. "Next to Constancia, you'll look like somebody out on parole." Frowning slightly, she slipped into an ankle-length pool topper of the same material and then looked happier at the finished effect. That outfit had caused havoc with her clothes budget; with any luck it should have the same effect at the poolside.

She dropped her room key in her robe pocket and tucked her swim cap and a towel under her arm before letting herself out on the deserted veranda. The muffled sound of voices and laughter made her peek over the balcony railing. Chris and Kent were already in the pool and Constancia was stretched out on a nearby lounge, her tanned limbs showing to full advantage in a white bikini.

Amanda's movement on the veranda must have caught Kent's attention because he gestured and called, "Come on down! We've been waiting for you."

She waved in return and nodded. As she made her way to the stairs, she decided it was kind of him to sound concerned. Unlike some other people she could mention.

The one she had in mind pulled himself out of the pool as she approached. He gave her a measuring look as he reached for a towel. Clearly he hadn't forgotten the circumstances under which they'd parted, nor had his temper improved in the interval. "I thought you'd decided to go into seclusion."

"Not today." Amanda put her towel and swim cap on a chair at a safe distance from him. "It took me a while to get organized."

"You must be perishing for something cool," Kent contributed from the middle of the pool where he was floating on his back. "I can recommend the gin and tonic."

"There are plenty of other things to choose from," Constancia swung her feet to the ground and picked up her own empty glass. "It will be quicker to help ourselves than ring for one of the boys. They're usually busy in the kitchen now. Just follow me." She led the way down one of the paths to a tiny bar fitted into a room by the screened dining room. "What would you like?" she asked, moving behind the counter.

"Gin and tonic will be fine, thank you." Amanda said politely. "You have a beautiful home here. The gardens are really magnificent."

Constancia nodded, intent on dropping ice in a tall glass. "We like it. When we changed it to a guest house, it wasn't as bad as Miguel and I thought it would be. We always had crowds of people around when we were growing up. Now. . ." Her lovely shoulders went up in a Latin shrug, "we simply get paid for it."

"Miguel's your brother?"

"That's right." Constancia floated a slice of lime on the drink and put it up on the counter. She nodded toward a framed picture of a man in his mid-twenties which was hanging on the wall nearby. "That photograph was taken last month. It's too bad you won't meet him—but he was called to Guadalajara on business the day before yesterday."

"I'm sorry, too." Amanda went over to study the picture more closely. "He's very nice-looking," she added with perfect truth.

"Don't think that he doesn't know it," Constancia said wryly. "Miguel is the reason we have such a long guest list at the Hacienda. You'd think women would give up when they don't receive any encouragement," she added in the complacent tone of a woman untroubled with that misfortune. She added a splash of soda to her highball glass and came around the end of the counter. "I must say that Kent Ives is a pleasant surprise. From his letter, I thought he was just another stodgy businessman."

"He seems very nice," Amanda fell into step beside her as they went outdoors again. "Of course, I hardly know him. What *is* his business exactly?"

"He has a chain of gift stores in Florida. Very successful ones, I gather. He's thinking of adding some of our Hacienda Handicrafts." She smoothed back her black hair which fell thickly over her tanned shoulders. "It could be a big new market for us."

"I'd enjoy seeing your workshop if it's possible.

Chris told me how successful you've been using the village labor."

A satisfied smile played around Constancia's mouth. "Chris has been wonderful ... giving me advice ... letting me lean on him ..."

Amanda's lips tightened at the implication.

"José thought the world of him," Constancia went on. Her voice flattened suddenly. "I suppose he's told you about José's disappearance?"

"Yes. I'm terribly sorry. It must be dreadful—not knowing what really happened."

"It's been like a nightmare. Last week I thought it was finally over, and as terrible as the news was, it was a relief to hear something definite." She stopped in the middle of the path. "Can you understand that?"

"Of course." Amanda's tone was quiet. "It sounds very normal. After all this time, you must have been expecting something like that."

The other nodded. "The authorities have decided that a wild animal killed the man whose body was found. It happens around here; wounded jaguars have turned on village hunters before this. But José would have been more careful." Her fingers tightened on her glass until the knuckles showed white with strain. "I wish he'd given up his silly ideas about hoping to find Mayan treasure. If only he'd tried to get interested in our work at the Hacienda, he would have found as much satisfaction. And we'd have been married by now, instead of living this day-by-day existence." Her face crumpled. "Oh, what's the use!"

"I'm terribly sorry," Amanda began awkwardly, wishing she could offer some real comfort. "This must have been a terrible experience for you." She saw Chris watching before getting up to stride toward them. "Maybe Chris can unearth something now that he's here."

Constancia brought her head up and managed a thin smile. "I certainly hope so."

He pulled up in front of them, still in his damp swimming trunks but with a matching navy-blue shirt thrown over his shoulders. It hung open and drew Amanda's fascinated gaze to his broad tanned chest until she managed to concentrate on the towel he was rubbing over his wet hair. "You look upset," he accused Constancia. "Is something wrong?"

"Just the same old thing." She put out a helpless hand and Amanda saw it disappear in his strong masculine one. Constancia rested her forehead against his shoulder for a moment before straightening and saying, "When you're around—I have so many memories. José was always talking about you and the good times we had."

"Excuse me, please," Amanda murmured as she pushed past them and put her glass on a low table. Being an unwanted onlooker at any time was awkward and this was proving worse than usual. She was happy to don her petalled swim cap and go over to the deep end of the pool where Kent was sunning himself on a rubber mattress.

"Do I hear the patter of tiny feet?" he murmured without opening his eyes. "This is faster service than I imagined."

"What did you want?"

"Well, I asked for a troupe of dancing girls," he said, settling himself more comfortably, "but one will do."

"Any special routine you prefer?" she asked sweetly.

"I'll tell you after I've seen your repertoire." He stretched and gave her a mocking grin. "Just a second until I push this mattress around so the light isn't in my eyes."

"Don't bother. Let me help." Amanda crouched for a dive from the side of the pool. There was a slight splash as her body entered the water and the next minute she had reached the mattress and neatly tipped him off it.

Kent's head bobbed to the surface almost immediately and he scooped a handful of water over her. "I *thought* that would get you in. Things were getting dull around here."

"You just need some exercise," Amanda said, happy for any interruption which would make her forget the other couple still huddled in the middle of the path. "What about a game of tag?"

"I can think of better games," Kent replied with a wicked glint in his eye, "but they might get us thrown out of the country." He looked over his shoulder and saw Constancia and Chris start strolling back to the poolside. Turning back to Amanda, he said, "You're *it*!" as he put a large hand on the top of her head and proceeded to duck her thoroughly.

Amanda came up sputtering but the next ten minutes were exhilarating fun as they covered the pool's surface. Kent was the stronger swimmer although Amanda's slim figure proved more elusive in the tight turns. The match was finally declared a draw when both of them staggered up the steps at the shallow end of the pool and collapsed on the sunwarmed tiles.

"I should think you'd be exhausted after that. Most of our guests don't even get in the pool," Constancia said from her chaise longue. Chris was lighting a cigarette in a canvas chair at her side.

"Have to find some exercise after sitting around

all day," Kent replied. "That's the worst part of traveling. A man goes numb on both ends after a few days of it." He stood up and went over to sit in a chair by Chris. "Mind if I bum a cigarette?"

"Help yourself," the other said tersely.

Kent did so and then, as a polite afterthought, offered the package to Amanda. "How about you, partner?"

"No, thank you." She took off her swim cap and shook out her hair. "Maybe you can do some exploring tomorrow for exercise—or have you planned a fishing trip?"

"I'll have to tend to business in the morning," Kent said after lighting his cigarette and replacing the package on the table with a nod of thanks. "Too bad your brother isn't here," he added to Constancia.

"It won't make the slightest bit of difference. We're equal partners in the Handicraft Center so I can answer your questions just as well."

"That's better still. Maybe I'll even have time for a drive to Chichen Itza in the afternoon. It'd be a shame to miss it after coming all the way to Yucatán."

"Are you interested in Mayan ruins?" Constancia sounded as if she was merely being polite.

"Only as a tourist." Kent got up to retrieve a glass of beer that he'd placed carefully in the shade. "I'm a lot more interested in the sport fishing off the coast."

"At least you're honest . . ."

"You bet." He took a long swallow, sighed with satisfaction and sat back down in his chair. "Of course, everybody's heard about Chichen Itza so I thought I'd take a quick look at the Well of the Maidens and that ball court where the members of the losing team lost their heads." He shook his own reflectively. "And to think they're complaining about player conditions in the football leagures *these* days."

A look of amusement passed over Chris's stern features. "I heard recently that the members of the winning team on that ball court lost their heads—even battled for the honor. That's what you call player incentive!"

Kent's eyebrows went up. "No wonder the Mayan race finally vanished. What with tossing their maidens in the wells of sacrifice and people lining up to put their heads under the guillotine . . ."

"On the sacrificial stones . . ." Amanda corrected.

"Okay—on the sacrificial stones. It's a wonder they managed to hang on for even a generation."

"You're not doing them justice, you know," Chris told him. "In 320 A.D. the Mayas had a calendar more accurate than the one we use today. They'd probably been perfecting it for a couple of centuries before that. You can't overestimate their civilization."

"I'm surprised there's so much hearsay about them and so few facts," Kent replied, serious for a change.

"That's easy to explain." Constancia pushed up on an elbow as she gestured at the tropical garden around them. "Look at the vegetation in this part of the country. If we walked away and left the Hacienda tomorrow, the buildings would be completely hidden in five years. You can imagine what happens to ruins."

Chris nodded. "Thank god for the big things like pyramids and the *sacbe—*"

"*Sacbe?*" Amanda asked, puzzled.

His glance moved her way. "That's right. *Sacbe—*another word for the white roads . . . the elevated highways which connected the Mayan cities. They're still found in parts of the jungle. At one time they were considered holy, so every traveler was safe from being molested. Nobody knows why the Mayas moved north from Guatemala to here. The climate's terrible in this country," he shot an apologetic glance at Constancia. "And there isn't a single bit of running water except for the damned sinkholes."

"No rivers or streams?" Amanda sounded incredulous.

"Not a one," Constancia confirmed. "They depended on the holes for their main water supply. Frankly I don't know how they stood it. They're terrible moldy things."

"You'd have thought they would have dug wells for irrigation during the dry season," Kent said.

"Well, they didn't—as far as anybody knows," Chris said. He was watching Amanda's profile. "What's bothering you?"

She was surprised at his perception. "I don't know. Just the thought of women and children being thrown in those smelly old sinkholes to honor the rain god Chac—and then using that same water for drinking and laundry." She shuddered visibly.

He stood up and tossed her robe to her without comment.

"I'm not cold," Amanda protested. "It was a 'walking over a grave' feeling."

"Put it on, anyhow," he was buttoning his shirt as he spoke. "That breeze feels good, but there's no sense in your getting chilled."

Amanda was surprised to see the palm trees moving over their heads and she obediently slipped her arms into the robe. "The cooler air feels wonderful. I hope it lasts a while."

"It should make your room more comfortable." Constancia got to her feet. "We might as well get dressed for dinner. The boys try to serve promptly at seven thirty."

"Are there any other guests?" Amanda asked.

The other woman shook her head as she picked up her own robe. "Not until next weekend. After the winter season here, all of us need a rest."

"Then I feel doubly honored." Kent slung a towel around his shoulders and worked his feet into a pair of thongs as he got ready to leave with the rest. "You should have written that this was your holiday time."

Constancia gave him a slow smile. "There's always time for business. Miguel and I have been wanting a good Florida outlet for years."

"That doesn't sound like the Mexican 'mañana' theory I've been reading about," Kent said as they started up the path.

Constancia laughed. "How many of our people have you seen sleeping in the sun with sombreros over their eyes?" She gestured toward the balcony where a maid was carrying an armful of ironed linen and a man was industriously wet-mopping the tiled floor.

"You mean I shouldn't believe all I read in the papers?" Kent replied with a chuckle. "Fair enough. I'll be ready to go through your shop first thing in the morning."

"Maybe you'd like to look over the shop, as well," Chris murmured to Amanda. "I can arrange it if you like."

She slowed to let the other couple go ahead. "What are you going to do?"

"If you must know, I'm going to scout around the area where José was working. It's probably a wild-goose chase but I'm curious."

It didn't take long for Amanda to juggle the possibilities offered to her. "That sounds more interesting than looking at pottery vases and watching people weaving. I'd rather go with you ... even if I have to sit in the car part of the time."

He tried to hang onto his patience. "Look, Amanda—use your head. That country isn't like Chichen Itza where they've got an air-conditioned restaurant six blocks from the pyramids. It's a jeep trip with the last part through the underbrush after the trail runs out. You'll be better off here." He started to move ahead.

Amanda caught at his shirttail. "I don't care where I'd be 'better off.' It's going to look pretty silly if you go off for the day leaving your 'fiancée' cooling her heels in the pool. I might even mention it at the dinner table—about how you're going to search for a hidden tomb."

"Constancia already knows," he told her in an icy tone. "But I'd just as soon not have it telegraphed around the countryside." His thick eyebrows hooded his glance as he stared down at her. "I don't suppose it would do any good to use a little blackmail of my own."

Amanda took a prudent step backward. "Not a bit. There must be other jeeps for hire and Kent could be persuaded to go for a drive in the country rather than joining the tourists at Chichen Itza in the afternoon."

"A drive in the country," Chris repeated scornfully. "Damned if it wouldn't serve you right—" he broke off and tossed his towel over his shoulder as if he'd come to a sudden decision. "All right, Amanda. We'll play it your way. Bring your pith helmet *and* a gallon of mosquito repellent . . ."

Her jaw dropped but she tried to recover quickly. "What time are we leaving?"

"Right after breakfast. I've ordered room service for five thirty," he announced calmly.

Amanda tried not to wince as she calculated. That meant getting up at five so she could be dressed by the time food arrived. From Chris's smug expression, she figured the early departure time had been recently decided. Probably in the last thirty seconds.

"All right," she said finally. "I'll be ready. Can Junior come along?"

"Good god almighty." Chris closed his eyes as if hoping for celestial assistance. "Are you sure you don't have a Cub Scout group you want to bring, too?"

"You needn't be sarcastic."

He clutched at his hair and then made a grab for his towel as it slipped from his shoulder. "Look, Amanda—if there's anything Junior doesn't need at this point, it's a run in the woods. I'll see that Pablo keeps an eye on him tomorrow so you can stop frowning."

"Make sure it's a close watch." As they continued to the stairs, Amanda saw a flutter of wings and watched Guaca clamber onto an iron perch in a flower bed. The parrot gave her a baleful glance as she skirted around him. Clearly he hadn't forgotten his rout when they had arrived. "I think he hates all of us," she muttered. "And Junior most of all."

Chris urged her on up the stairs. "Junior can take care of himself. He's got teeth like a crocodile, but he doesn't seem to have figured out what they're for. I hope I'm not around when he does." He pulled up when he reached the doorway to her room and looked over his shoulder. "Where did Ives go? I thought he was headed this way."

"Constancia probably took him on a shortcut," Amanda found her key and inserted it in the lock.

"Are you going to tell him about the trip tomorrow?"

"Only in a general way." Chris absently whacked his towel against his thigh. "If he takes you strolling in the garden tonight and asks questions, remember to keep your mouth shut. Do you understand?"

"How could I miss after you put it so delicately?" Amanda was wishing she could transfer the towel up to his stubborn neck in a slip knot. He'd kept her on the defensive ever since they'd arrived.

"That's exactly what I intended," he said, reading her thoughts again. "If you insist on dealing yourself into the game, you're going to have to play it my way." He started on down the veranda, adding, "Set your alarm tonight. I don't think you'd like the way I'd get you out of bed." His tone turned caustic. "And I damned well don't plan to hang around waiting for you."

Amanda managed to get inside her room and close the door without slamming it; it was an effort but it was a small triumph as well. For that she was grateful.

She was also well aware it was the only triumph she'd managed all day.

Chapter Five

Amanda needed a good night's sleep to help her forget the frustration of the day and enable her to be a sparkling, intelligent companion at the crack of dawn.

Unfortunately, the ancient Mayan gods in the neighborhood were not in sympathy. Whether it was her criticism of their sacred waters earlier in the afternoon or whether they were merely amusing themselves at her expense would never be determined but the end result was conclusive; she only slept in fitful intervals throughout the interminable night.

Shortly before midnight, the electricity failed and the overhead fan promptly stopped revolving. Despite open louvers and screened windows, the room temperature shot up and Amanda's pajamas became a winding sheet rather than featherlight batiste. Outside the window, a flock of birds reporting for the swing shift decided to make a night of it. Amanda lay with her eyes wide open as she composed a letter of protest to the Audubon Society. When the songbirds were joined in chorus by a gaggle of geese in the pond below, she could only pull the pillow around her ears and moan slightly.

At three o'clock she heard a growl from next door and knew a moment's satisfaction as Junior was

shushed by an irritated masculine voice. Chris was
having his troubles, too.

When the Hacienda's kitchen crew started
straggling to work, laughing and chatting on the
path below her window, Amanda sat up in bed and
reached over to turn off the alarm. For a moment,
she thought of putting a note on Chris's door saying
that she'd changed her mind about spending the day
with him. Then she pressed her lips together stub-
bornly and swung her feet to the floor. With any
luck, she could sneak a nap in the jeep while he was
off exploring the countryside. In the meantime, she'd
hope that a cold shower and breakfast coffee would
have some effect so that Chris need never know she
felt like a marathon dancer on the fourth day running.

Chris's first comment when she met him in the
parking lot proved she was wrong again.

"You look terrible," he said irritably. "I thought
you'd have sense enough to go to bed last night and
get some sleep."

She surveyed his tall form, clad in cotton shirt and
slacks, as he leaned against the side of an old jeep.
Then she walked over to sit on the front fender next
to him. "First of all," she ticked off a finger carefully,
"going to bed at the Hacienda Melgar does not
necessarily mean that one goes to sleep. I don't know
if they charge extra for that bird chorus but I've
heard Wagnerian ensembles that didn't make half as
much noise." Indignation strengthened her tones.
"Not only that, I've slept in Turkish baths with
lower humidity and softer springs . . ." She broke off
her recital as he started to chuckle and her lips
twitched reluctantly in response. "Pay no attention
to me," she said finally. "I could quarrel with the
Mona Lisa this morning."

"Come join the party," he said. "At least you didn't have Junior's hot breath on your ankles all night. Junior also suffers from insomnia. Either that or the thrill of sleeping under a roof was too good to miss. I don't think he closed an eye the whole damned night. What do you want to bet he sleeps all day in Pablo's hut?"

"Along with those miserable birds . . ." Amanda started to shake her aching head and then decided not to risk it. Instead she got up to walk around the jeep. "Did they buy this as surplus property after World War Two or the Battle of the Alamo?"

"I don't know but if Sam Houston gave it up, it was the smartest thing he ever did." Chris followed her around to the back of the ancient vehicle and kicked a tire morosely.

Her glance took in the ripped plastic seats and rusted fenders before fastening on the rear of the vehicle. "What's in that covered apple box tied on behind?"

"That apple box, madame, is the trunk. At the moment it has some odds and ends of tools. In five minutes more," he was surveying his watch, "it should also contain our lunch. Then we can get the hell out of here before the heat gets too fierce."

"Those clouds on the horizon look as if there'll be rain sometime today," Amanda commented. She glanced at a battered metal roof which was secured to the jeep by some pieces of rope and raised a questioning eyebrow.

"There's an old tarp in the back in case it gets very wet," Chris said reassuringly. He was surveying her low-heeled shoes, cotton skirt, and long-sleeved overblouse. "You'd better go back and get some kind of a hat for shade."

Amanda indicated her shoulder bag. "It's folded in here along with my sunglasses."

"You're sure you want to come along? All joking aside, this will be a rough trip."

"I know." Amanda was too tired to do more than agree with him. "But please let me, Chris. I promise not to bother you. Constancia and Kent have work to do today—they wouldn't want to look after me." She hesitated and then admitted frankly, "Besides, I'd rather be with you."

"From the way Kent hovered over you at dinner last night, I can't think he'd find chaperoning you any bother at all. But let's not argue about it," he added as she opened her lips to protest. "I'm not up to it this morning. Go on and get in the jeep, I see our lunch coming."

She clambered onto the torn passenger seat and watched him walk over to take a lunch basket from an amiable kitchen helper before storing it in the covered box behind the spare tire. After nodding his thanks to the waiter, he came around and slid onto the driver's seat. He rummaged around beside him and found a navy blue ski cap with a long visor, which he put on and pulled down to shade his eyes. Before putting the key in the ignition, he turned to Amanda. "All set?"

"I guess so." She was sitting up straight because she had no choice; refinements like arm rests and doors on the jeep had disappeared long ago. Two plastic jugs occupied the space between the two front seats.

Chris saw her eyes on them. "One's water—the other's coffee. Better hang onto that bar in front of you," he jerked his head toward the metal dashboard. "Otherwise I'll lose you at the first pothole."

"If Ralph Nader knew about this—he'd have a whole winter's work cut out for him."

Chris merely stepped on the starter and the engine came to life. The jeep went into reverse reluctantly with a crash of gears.

Amanda couldn't help smiling at his embarrassed reaction. "Grind me a pound while you're at it," she teased. "I thought you knew how to drive this thing."

His slow smile surfaced as he reached up to settle his cap more firmly on his head. "For that remark, madame, you'll pay dearly."

The first twenty miles were easy driving as they retraced part of their route from Mérida. Most of the activity was at the scattered roadside bus stops; already women were gathered in cheerful clusters anticipating their day's shopping in the capital. At the last stop, a teen-age girl was busily setting up her refreshment stand for the day by filling tall glasses with melon or pineapple.

Amanda gave Chris a questioning look as they drove past. "How do you drink watermelon?"

"Squash it with a wooden pestle as if you're making an ice cream soda. Afterwards, add sugar and water. Very tasty but don't try it here."

"Montezuma's revenge on the tourist," she murmured. "I'll remember."

Gradually, the land along the roadside presented a scorched appearance with stray palmettos turning yellow and sick-looking as they stood in the midst of the blackened soil.

"What's happened to all this?" Amanda asked as the damage followed the road for miles. "That's the strangest fire pattern I've ever seen."

"The farmers have cleared the land this way for centuries. Burn it off before the rainy season and then plant in June or July. Strictly subsistence-type agriculture," he went on, in response to her questioning look. "Corn, beans, melon, chile peppers, camotes . . ."

"You lost me on the last one . . ."

"And you an editor!" he mocked. "A sweet potato by any other name—"

"Is still a sweet potato." She was surveying the blackened landscape again. "It doesn't look like much but the people seem well fed. I shouldn't question the methods. Hey . . . what now?" She clutched at the dashboard as they turned off onto a gravel track.

"Now we leave civilization behind and you hang on tight." His tone was preoccupied as he tried to find the best route on the rutted surface. "We have another five miles of this and then it goes to dirt."

By the time the gravel on the road had disappeared, the farms had gone as well and the dirt track led directly into a dense undergrowth which barely cleared the sides of the jeep.

"Keep your arms inside," Chris barked after a thorny vine raked the back of Amanda's hand, leaving a bloody scratch in its wake. "There's a first-aid box on the floor behind you. Get some antiseptic on that . . . right now."

Amanda nodded and hung onto the back of the seat while she rummaged for a tube of antibiotic cream. Chris lowered the speed of the jeep as she applied it. "Okay, thanks." She replaced the medicine and faced front again. "How much farther is it?"

"Another five miles or so. It seems longer because of the damned potholes," he complained as the right front wheel jounced through one.

Amanda tried for a cheerful note. "It's like a television commercial for radial tires. You know, the kind where they drive over glass and spikes at fifty miles an hour and balance a cup of tea on the dashboard at the same time." She looked thoughtful. "Speaking of tea . . ."

"We'd better wait and have some when we get there. This road would be a damn sight worse after a downpour and I don't like the looks of the sky."

Amanda tried to peer up through the windshield and only succeeded in bumping her head in the attempt. "I thought it was the trees that made everything so gloomy. I've been expecting to see Tarzan or Jane swinging out at any minute."

Chris snorted. "It would have to be a short vine. Most of this growth isn't over thirty feet high. It's just the underbrush that closes everything in. Perfect browse for deer and other wildlife—that's why there's so much game around here."

"I'm glad those wild turkeys are the biggest things we've seen. Do you suppose there are any jaguars around?"

"Don't worry. Any sensible jaguar would make tracks in the opposite direction after he heard the cracked muffler on this jeep."

"You're probably lying like a trooper," Amanda said, considering, "but I appreciate it."

He smiled faintly. "Just because they found one victim in these parts doesn't mean that you have to be afraid of getting out of the car. Watch where you're walking though—there might be some snakes around."

"That does it!" Amanda looked resigned. "I'd rather face ten jaguars."

"Even one is highly unlikely. Besides, there's an abandoned hut fairly near the tomb excavations. José mentioned it to me." He stopped talking long enough to change gears in the middle of some deep ruts and then went on. "It might be the best place for you to wait."

"If you say so." Amanda looked undecided. "This seat isn't the lap of luxury but the dirt floor of a hut doesn't sound great either."

"It won't be that bad—there's a hammock underneath our lunch basket in the trunk. Whoever was driving this jeep believed in being prepared for his siesta."

"Would there be a place to put up a hammock in the hut," she asked skeptically.

"You bet! Down here, they find a place to put their hammocks right after the roof goes on. I'm just hoping there's some kind of stove, as well."

When they finally arrived at the small clearing with the hut on it, it was later than Chris had planned. He pulled over to the side of the track and turned off the jeep while Amanda stared at the desolate scene in front of them. Then her curious glance noted that the bushes lining the rough trail up to the hut had been trampled by recent visitors.

"Although I can't see why anybody would beat a path to that door," Amanda said, surveying the structure critically. "Whatever they're charging for rent is too much."

"I don't know why you're complaining, it's a real gem," Chris adopted the tone of a real estate salesman. "No utility bills, convenient floor plan, plenty of ventilation . . ."

"Not having any doors and windows helps on that." Amanda got out of the jeep stiffly, wondering if the circulation would ever come back to certain parts of her anatomy. She waited for Chris to come around the car and then followed him up the path to the dilapidated structure. After peering closely at its construction of vertical sticks reinforced with dried mud, she shook her head. "I don't see how it's lasted this long."

"The thatch roof helps," Chris told her as he led the way inside. "Besides, they have to make do with what they have. There isn't a lumber yard next door." He was looking around as he spoke. "This isn't too bad."

Amanda kept discreetly silent; she couldn't object to the hut's furnishings because there weren't any. Just a packed earth floor, exposed poles for rafters and a kind of fire pit on the far side under an opening which served as a window when it wasn't acting as a chimney.

"At least there's cross-ventilation," Chris said. "And I brought plenty of insect repellent."

She shuddered and then hoped that he hadn't noticed in the gloom of the hut's interior.

"Don't take it so seriously," he said, trying to reassure her. "We can have lunch in the car—then you can have a snooze in the hammock while I do some exploring."

"Of course ... it'll be fine," she agreed hastily. "But can't I see the tombs?"

"Sure—but they're just some holes in the ground." He led the way outside again and Amanda took a deep breath of relief.

"At least I can unpack the lunch," she said on the way back to the jeep. "If it's up to last night's standards, we're in for a treat."

Chris nodded and moved the covered basket up between the front seats after shoving the plastic jugs aside. "There we are—all the comforts of home. Don't take out more than you need," he added when she opened the lid. "There's a damned aggressive insect population around here and it doesn't need any encouraging."

"Oh, I didn't think . . ." Amanda delved into the basket once more, eventually handing out two neatly arranged platefuls of cold meat and cheese. "Plus two hard-boiled eggs." She explored the contents of the basket again and brought them triumphantly aloft.

"Anybody would think *you* were the one who was treasure hunting," Chris told her as he grinned and settled himself behind the steering wheel. "What is there that's liquid?"

"Beer," she told him after investigating. "Did you have a hand in that?"

"A small one." He took the bottle she gave him and reached for an opener. "There should be some lemonade, too. I wasn't sure what you wanted and it was too late to check when I put in the order last night. You'd already disappeared with Kent." He uncapped the beer and rested it against the basket. "What was on his mind? The usual things when a man takes a woman walking in the moonlight or was he just being curious?"

"If you *must* know, I was asking him about his gift shops in Florida," Amanda said. "Then he wanted to know about the publishing business and how I liked working with you."

"I won't ask any more . . ."

"You can stop fishing," she told him without looking up from the egg she was peeling. "I told him that you were temperamental but talented. Then he wanted to know how long I'd known you . . ."

"What did you say to that?"

"I made it sound as if we had adjoining cribs in the nursery." Amanda decided not to mention Kent's questions about their engagement.

Chris must have noticed her hesitation. "What happened then? Did he make a pass at you?"

"If you're so curious, you should have given me a tape recorder to take along." She tossed her hair back angrily. "He thinks we're engaged—Constancia told him that. He's too much of a gentlemen to make . . . overtures . . ."

"You can skip the two-syllable words." Chris took a swallow of beer and looked at her skeptically over the top of the bottle. "So he didn't try anything. I'll be damned . . ."

"With a mind like yours—that's quite possible." Amanda pulled a piece from her hard roll almost viciously. "*Some* men have minds that run in other directions."

"You might scrape up five or six guys like that in southern California, but I wouldn't count on it." His eyes narrowed as he stared through the windshield. "I wonder what Kent's game is?"

"Look—the man runs a chain of gift shops," Amanda began patiently. "After he finishes doing business with the Melgars, he hopes to get in a weekend of sport fishing at Isla or Cozumel—then he's going back home again. Nothing suspicious at all. Last night he was wondering if he could bend the wording on his apartment lease to accommodate Junior. He feels that he's his responsibility." She frowned down at the roll in her hand.

Chris's tone was casual. "I don't suppose you'd have much luck sneaking the pooch into your apartment in New York?"

For some reason, Amanda felt more depressed than ever. She shook her head. "Not the way things are, but I'll find some solution. He's certainly not going to stay here and roam the countryside again."

"Don't sound so fierce. These things work themselves out in time." Chris looked at his watch and then piled his empty plate back in the hamper. "I have to get going or I'll never get anything accomplished."

"I'm ready, too ... I can repack this later," Amanda stuffed her lunch remains into the basket and closed the lid. She watched Chris put a notebook into his pants pocket and check to make sure he had a small compass in his shirt.

"Put your hat on," he told her, getting out of the jeep. "I'll string the hammock so you can have someplace to rest when you come back to the hut."

Silently Amanda looked on as he reached into the storage box of the jeep and hauled out a maroon-colored hammock. She followed him as far as the open doorway of the hut and saw him examine the peeled pole supports inside before a look of satisfaction came over his face.

"I *told* you there'd be some hooks," he said over his shoulder as he affixed the net loops at either end, leaving the hammock swaying three feet above the dirt floor. "There you are—all the comforts of home. Now, we can be on our way."

Outside again, she saw him pause at the corner of the hut, remove the compass from his pocket, and, after checking the scribbled page of his notebook, take a sighting on a gray chicle tree which stood higher than the rest.

"So we can get home again," he said when he was finished. "I'd hate to be late for dinner."

She shivered suddenly although the humid air was oppressively hot. "Don't even mention the thought."

Amanda kept at his side for the first five minutes of their trek through the underbrush and then she fell behind, squaw-fashion, for protection from the clinging bushes and unexpected pitfalls on the rocky ground. Fallen branches and leaves made the footing uncertain, especially when they moved through a swampy area where the ground hadn't dried from the last rain. At one point, she glanced upward through the branches of a flamboyant tree as if checking the weather.

Chris saw her do it. "If that downpour holds off for a couple of hours, it should give us plenty of time. And once we get away from the hut, the track is rocky enough for traction even in the rain."

"I wasn't thinking of us," Amanda said truthfully. "I was just wondering how any relics survived in this area. It's almost a bog despite the vegetation."

"You'll understand how the Mayas coped with the water table when you see their tombs." He was checking his compass and his notes as they came to a small rocky hillock. "This must be the first one," he said in a tone of satisfaction. "José said it had been discovered about ten years ago. Come over here and I'll show you how they lined their work to protect the burial chamber."

Amanda stumbled behind him over to what appeared to be a simple hole in the ground. At his urging, she bent down to examine the interior and found a cavity approximately eight feet long, three feet wide, and almost four feet deep. As in the Mayan pyramids, the stone walls of the tomb slanted together at the ceiling and were joined by a capstone to seal the gap. Native stone had been used throughout and was laboriously fitted in rectangular pieces, the masonry done so well that no grouting was needed between the blocks to keep them in place. Even hundreds of years later, the stone frame was in almost pristine condition.

When Amanda marveled at this, Chris merely nodded. "Unfortunately the stonework's the only thing left to admire. Sometimes archaeologists discover a few bones in these but looters have always taken everything else. That's why José was so excited about his find. Imagine an untouched tomb with a prize like those golden disks . . ." Chris shook his head. "It was Shangri La, Valhalla, and the Rhinegold all rolled into one."

"And that tomb is close by?"

"Not too far—from what I've figured out."

Amanda's attention was caught by a hole in the center of one of the stones close to the ceiling arch. "That looks as if it's been made deliberately."

Chris brought his attention back with an obvious effort. "I forgot that you didn't know about those. The Mayans didn't neglect their hammocks even in the old times; it was their custom to put the body in a hammock and then surround it with tributes and utensils the victims could use in after-life. These are similar to the Egyptian tombs in that respect." He shoved his hands in his pockets. "Had enough?"

She nodded and stood upright again. "Yes, thanks." Then, with an appealing glance at him from under her lashes, "Can't I go along with you? Honestly, I wouldn't be any trouble."

Chris reached over to flick her chin companionably. "Sorry, Amanda—not this time. I have a lot of ground to cover and your legs aren't long enough. Not that I don't approve of them just the way they are," he added with a slow grin, "but they're not the right models for going cross-country. Come on, let's get you back to the hut."

Amanda started to say that she could find her way back by herself but, after a quick glance around, followed meekly in his tracks. "Do you have any kind of a map for that cache of José's?" she asked as he paused to push aside an overhanging branch.

"Just the bare bones of one," Chris said over his shoulder. "I wish now that José had been more explicit when he talked at the airport. Of course, then, secrecy was all the thing. He and his partner were determined to keep everything under wraps until they had the disks safely excavated."

Amanda grimaced. "Back to that missing partner again. It's the one part of José's behavior that doesn't make sense."

"I know. Especially being so close-mouthed about it with his own family. They knew somebody was helping to finance his exploration but that's all. After José disappeared, they hoped the partner would surface but after all these months with no leads . . ."

"It sounds like the missing partner is the prime suspect," Amanda finished. "Otherwise, he would be as anxious as everyone else to help. Oh, damn!" She winced with pain as her foot slipped on a dead branch and would have fallen if Chris hadn't whirled and caught her.

"Okay?" he wanted to know as she regained her balance.

She waggled her foot and decided it was still in working order before sighing with relief, "Yes—thanks."

"Then hang on to me and watch where you put your feet." He took a firm clasp on her left hand and threaded his fingers through hers. "I'm not in the mood for an emergency drive to the nearest hospital."

Amanda walked on meekly, aware of a comfortable warmth brought about by his closeness. Unfortunately, she was so aware of it that all other parts of that enforced march back to the hut fused into nothingness and she was astounded when the structure suddenly emerged in front of them.

Chris dropped her hand with a promptness that was scarcely flattering. "Okay, you're on your own," he told her. "Go in and take a nap or read a book or something but *don't*," he practically growled the word, "start wandering around. I want to be ready to leave in a hurry when I get back and I'll expect to find you either in that hammock or the jeep. Here ..." he fumbled in his shirt pocket, "I'll leave the key for the jeep just in case ..."

"... in case of what?" she asked, forgetting any annoyance in the light of this bigger threat. "You don't think there's a chance of *your* getting lost, do you? Because if you do, I'm coming with you ..."

"Then we could both be lost together! That makes a hell of a lot of sense," he said with a disgusted look. "Just go in there and count mosquitoes or something before I lose my temper and push you in the nearest sinkhole." He sent her on her way with a firm slap on her backside. "Keep the beer in the shade—I'll be thirsty when I get back." Then he turned and was gone through the underbrush before she could think of a properly scathing reply.

Reluctantly, she peered in the hut. The gloomy interior looked just as discouraging as she remembered; the hammock swaying slightly as she touched it, the air as musty and still as a seaside cabin in winter. For a moment she thought of trying to relax on the woven hammock but a glance at the thatched roof with its possible inhabitants made her escape back outside. She got in the jeep and pulled off her hat with a sigh. The car's interior might be dusty but it didn't harbor any lurking scorpions or snakes. She rummaged to find a collapsible cup in her handbag and poured herself a drink from the water jug. The first swallow of the heavily chlorinated water made her wrinkle her nose but she drank it down to the last drop and then carefully recapped the jug. After she'd replaced her cup, she looked at her watch, thinking that Chris wouldn't be back for an hour or so at the best. If she finished the paperback novel she'd tucked in her purse, the time might go faster and she could ignore the mosquito that was even now humming around her right ear.

It was a testimonial to the book's plot that Amanda was able to forget both the time and the discomfort of her surroundings for a while. When the first raindrops struck her wrist it took her a moment or two to come back to reality. She blinked like someone emerging from a deep sleep as she stuck her head out from under the protection of the metal roof to see what was happening. Not surprisingly, she received a spatter of raindrops full in the face as she discovered that the dark clouds which had been on the horizon had covered the entire sky with a gray shroud. Even as she stared, the rumble of thunder forecast what was to come.

Amanda ducked back under cover and frowned as she checked her watch. It had been over two hours since Chris had left! Another rumble of thunder and the increasing volume of rain on the roof made her pull away from her side of the jeep where the moisture was starting to blow in. At the same time, she noticed rivulets of moisture start collecting on the soft ground beside the car. What was it Chris had said about wanting to get the jeep onto firmer ground before the rain started?

She reached into her pocket and brought out the car key he'd given her, bouncing it uncertainly in her palm while she tried to decide what was best to do. Then she shrugged and pushed herself over the gap between the bucket seats to settle behind the steering wheel.

Her scowl deepened as she leaned forward to fit the key into the ignition switch on the dashboard.

The driver's seat was so far back that her toe barely reached the accelerator and so low that her vision was obscured by the top of the steering wheel. Without some sort of cushion, she felt like a toddler sitting in an adult chair at a restaurant. Chris would rock with laughter if he could see her.

That thought made her expression all the more determined. With any luck, she could get the jeep turned around and safely out on the rocky track past the clearing before he appeared.

The prospect of his gratified expression when he heard about her accomplishment made her shelve any qualms. After all, she had driven a foreign sports car one weekend in Connecticut. The jeep couldn't be more difficult.

She turned on the key and reached for the starter with her toe, after prudently making sure the gearshift was in neutral. The engine started almost immediately, sounding like the roar of a jet plane in the shrouded emptiness. Amanda looked around once again; surely the sound of the motor would bring Chris running if he were close by. When nothing happened, she stretched out at full length with her chin resting against the steering wheel as she gunned the accelerator with her toe. If she could only move the driver's seat forward . . .

She fumbled at the front and side of the seat for a lever to change its position, but without any luck. "Damn!" she muttered and pulled herself up a fraction to survey the weather outside. The occasional raindrops settled down to the expected deluge even as she watched. There was no doubt about it—the ground around the jeep wheels would be in quagmire state within half an hour at the rate the water was coming down.

She leaned out again to check that the space behind her was clear. By making the tightest turn possible, she could avoid the even-softer ground in front of the hut. Carefully, she depressed the clutch with her left foot while she used both hands on the gearshift to pull it into reverse. There was a clash of metal as the gearshift protested her ministrations before settling into place. Now ... all she had to do was turn the wheel and let up slowly on the clutch ...

She was so intent on cramping the stubborn steering column that her release of the clutch pedal wasn't the gentle motion she had hoped for. In fact, she'd barely lifted her shoe when the car took off in a series of spastic lurches; not backward as she'd planned so carefully—but forward.

The bark of a gum tree was skinned with the right fender on the first lurch, a pigeon was sent squawking on the second. Then the hood plunged and stuck in the prickly undergrowth before the roar of the engine mercifully died away.

Chapter Six

It all happened so fast that when it was over, Amanda found herself still clutching the steering wheel—only this time with a smarting forehead which had collided with the horn button at the final moment. As she sat there trembling, she abruptly became aware of a noise other than the dinning of the rain on the metal roof.

"Amanda! Amanda, are you all right?" The thorny vines encasing the jeep sides rustled and then parted as a masculine arm pushed through ... followed by a familiar masculine countenance.

Even in her confusion, Amanda was able to note the changing expressions on Chris's face. Initial concern was replaced by relief as he saw her still upright and then exasperation took over as he turned to survey the jeep's resting place.

"What in the merry hell did you try to do?" There was an icy wedge as wide as a canoe paddle between each word. "Five feet more and you could have harvested a chicle tree all by yourself."

Amanda let go of the steering wheel and rubbed her forehead irritably, wondering if she'd be branded by a horn ring for the rest of her days. "I was trying to turn the jeep around so it wouldn't get stuck in that soft ground when something went wrong," she informed him with considerable hauteur. "If you'd gotten back on time before this rain started, it wouldn't have been necessary." She was watching the water run down the bridge of his nose with perverse satisfaction.

Chris was so angry that he was unaware of the man-made waterfall. "You don't have to take the Great Circle route every time you turn around, for god's sake. Why didn't you stay in the clear?"

"I planned to. Can I help it if Mexican gearshifts are backwards?"

He snorted. "Mexican? This thing was assembled in Detroit."

"You're crazy," she told him flatly. "I drove a sports car last summer and I didn't have any trouble shifting."

"A European sports car, I suppose." Chris sounded resigned.

"Why, yes—since you mention it." Realization hit her. "You mean they're different?"

"By now, I should think you could write a book on it." He was peering down at the tires as he spoke. "This side looks whole. Maybe I can still move it." He beckoned impatiently. "Come on—out! Every minute we waste, that ground's getting softer . . ."

"I know." She clambered from the driver's side with difficulty and felt the full force of the rain for the first time.

"Here . . . get under this." Chris pulled a tarp from the box on the back bumper and draped it over her head and shoulders. "There's no point in your getting soaked."

"What about you? Your shirt's already sticking to you."

"I'll take it off later." He slid into the driver's seat and reached for the key. "You go on back to the hut. This is apt to take a while."

"All right." She added reluctantly, "I think the right front wheel sort of . . . hit something . . . at the very last. Don't look like that . . . I didn't do it deliberately."

Chris rubbed his forehead with the back of his hand. "I know. Look, Amanda—go on in and get out of the rain."

"But maybe I could help push or something . . ."

"If you don't get out of here, I'll have you digging trenches with your fingernails," he threatened and started the noisy motor before she could answer.

It was fully fifteen minutes later before his figure loomed in the doorway of the hut, his arms laden with a jacket, the lunch basket, and other assorted gear.

"What's all that for?" she asked faintly.

"Amenities to speed the passing hours," he said, going over to deposit them by the fire pit. "I noticed earlier that this place needed some home comforts. The furnishing is strictly Morgue Modern at the moment."

Amanda brushed that aside. "You mean you can't move the jeep?" she asked, going to the heart of the matter.

"Not until the rain stops and that ground dries a little. I thought I'd better give up before I got deeper than the wheel hubs or we'd be here all summer." He shoved his hands in his pockets and surveyed the interior of the hut. "This could be worse—at least the roof doesn't leak."

Amanda nodded and shrugged out from under the tarp.

"Here, I'll take that," Chris said. "If we throw it over one of these poles, it'll have a chance to dry." He was spreading it on an exposed roof beam. Once he'd finished, he looked around and scowled as a gust of rain swept in the doorway, causing Amanda to shudder.

She wrapped her arms around her breast and managed to grin when she noted his concern. "Too bad the carpenter left before he put on the door. Somebody should complain to the Housing Commission." She kept her voice casual. "How long will we have to stay?"

He hunched his shoulders and went over to peer through the doorway at the stormy sky. "This won't blow over until the middle of the night and then the ground will need some hours to drain. I'd say we might have a chance by breakfast time—providing the sun comes out." He turned back into the room, ignoring her stricken silence. "Fortunately we still have some food in the basket so we won't starve. Now I'd better get a fire going and dry things out."

"You'll have to take off that wet shirt," Amanda murmured, trying to sound equally matter-of-fact. Inwardly, her thoughts were churning as she contemplated spending the night in that desolate place. Of course Chris was right; she should be grateful for the shelter. And he was decent enough not to remind her of her *faux pas* with the jeep. She looked at his broad shoulders as he rummaged in the crude fire pit and said again, "I thought you were going to get out of that shirt."

"In a minute. I'll have to go out and get some wood to burn so it won't hurt if I get a little wetter. It's a good thing there are some half-burned sticks here for kindling. It'd be a rough haul with just wet wood." He stood up and brushed his pants absently. "I'd better go now before it gets any darker."

"For heaven's sake, put on the tarp," she said as he started for the door. "You'll be absolutely drenched otherwise."

He started to protest and then gave in with a grin. "Okay . . . but I don't plan to go far." He wrapped the nylon cover around him, as he added, "You can root through that lunch basket and decide on the dinner menu. At the moment, I'd trade the cold beer for a mug of soup."

"Make that two mugs and I'm with you."

He nodded. "Well, wish me luck. At this rate, we may spend the night rubbing two sticks together."

Amanda watched him disappear through the door and went over to drag the lunch basket closer to the opening at the rear of the hut to utilize the fading light.

By the time she finished making an inventory of their food, she felt doubly discouraged. Undoubtedly things would look better once Chris got a fire going, but even Julia Child wouldn't get excited about a menu consisting of rolls, hard-boiled eggs, two oranges, and some bottles of beer.

When Chris came stamping in a few minutes later, he found her morosely huddled on the edge of the hammock, hugging her arms for warmth. "About to freeze? Never fear . . . help is here!" He gave her an outrageous grin and went over to the fire pit to disgorge the load of branches he was protecting under his tarp. "Now—if I can just remember how I got that firemaker's merit badge in the Boy Scouts fifteen years ago . . ."

Amanda got up to look over his shoulder. "If you need anybody for huffing and puffing, I'm happy to volunteer."

"I'll make a note of it." Chris was assembling his dry embers carefully and added some crumpled pages from his notebook. "Now—let's see if we can baby it along," he said, reaching for his lighter.

The flame flared and then caught hold for a

steady burning in the collection of moss, shaved bark, and embers. Chris watched it intently, piling on small branches first and finally, when the fire was thoroughly established—the larger ones.

Amanda held her hands out to the warmth almost greedily. "Oh—it feels wonderful! I wasn't really cold—just sort of damp around the edges—but this makes all the difference."

"At least, it's a step in the right direction. I'll make another trip out to the jeep and see if there's anything we overlooked."

"Like a T-bone steak?" Amanda suggested hopefully.

"More like a can of beans. If we really wanted to practice survival tactics, we could try for some game . . ."

"Oh, no! I'll huff and puff . . . but that's as far as I go. Cleaning game is not part of the service."

Chris was looking amused as he stood up and pulled the tarp around his shoulders once again. "A fine pioneer woman you'd have made."

"I know. If it had depended on me—the westward movement in America would never have gotten beyond the Appalachians." She brushed back her hair. "If you wanted a back-to-nature partner, you should have brought along that man who eats wild hickory nuts on television."

"You'll do, but watch that fire. If you let it go out, I'll send you out in the rain for the next load of wood."

Amanda looked after his figure until it disappeared into the underbrush and then turned back to the fire as he instructed. Her lips curved with amusement but she had no doubts that he meant exactly what he said.

He was elated when he came back a few minutes

later. "I *told* you there might be something rolling around in the back of that jeep," he said, holding up a can of food in one hand and the plastic water jug in the other. "How would you like beans for dinner?"

"I'd *love* beans for dinner," she said quite truthfully. "Should I ask what kind of beans?"

"Damned if I know. From what's left of the label, I think they're red ones!" He tossed her the can and fished in his back pocket. "Look what else I dredged from under the seat!" He held up a grimy white candle. "It's dinner by candlelight. Nothing but the best."

"Hallelujah! All the comforts of home. Too bad you didn't unearth a color television set, too."

He shook his head as he wedged the candle into the notch of an overhead beam. "Don't press your luck. This is the first find I've made today. I might as well have saved myself the trip this afternoon."

"I was going to ask you but I was so busy wrecking the jeep that it slipped my mind." She watched him use a blade on his pocket knife to open the beans before putting the can at the edge of the fire. After he'd finished, she went on gently, "I can see where that maneuver must have been the final blow on a lovely afternoon."

He grinned and started to unbutton his shirt. "Something like that. I hope you don't mind if I use the rope on the hammock as a clothesline for a while. Where in the devil did I put my jacket?"

She went over to the back wall and retrieved it. "When in Yucatán, look on the floor first."

"Just like home. Thanks." He shrugged into it and then glanced over quizzically, "Maybe you need this more than I do?"

"Not since you lit that fire." She noticed the lines

of weariness at the corners of his eyes and mouth as he moved closer to the flames. "You look as if you've just about had it."

"Food will help. I'm getting too old to run around on half-baked treasure-hunts."

"Maybe you were expecting too much. After all, José didn't give you explicit directions."

He raised an exasperated face. "That's the worst of it. I'm pretty sure I was in the right area, but when I got to the place where the tomb should have been, there was just some disturbed earth. If there had been a tomb there, somebody had very cleverly removed all traces of it."

"Weren't there even any rocks left?

"Use your head, woman! Of course there were rocks. There are so many rocks in this country it could practically double as a gravel pit. But I wanted to find some still lining a tomb."

"You're snapping my head off again," she reminded him.

"Sorry . . ." His grin was reluctant. "I could go over and beat *my* head against the wall instead."

"For heaven's sake—don't! The whole place would fall down around us." Her expression sobered as she thought about the tomb. "It's strange that Constancia doesn't know more. After all, she and José were engaged to be married."

"That doesn't make any difference. This is Mexico and there's still a wide gap between the sexes. Constancia is allowed to handle handicrafts at the Hacienda but even that's pretty daring for this part of the country. As for archaeology . . ." he shook his head. "Not a chance. José wanted to surprise her when he found those disks."

"You mean . . . to 'come bearing gifts'?"

"Something like that." Chris shrugged. "Is it so

strange? Most men are part exhibitionist when it comes to the woman they love. José just wanted to do it his way." His expression grew bleak. "Only he disappeared before he could."

There was a moment of silence as they both stared into the fire, intent on their thoughts.

Then Amanda asked, "What do you do now? Give up or try another tack?"

He raised his hands and stretched lazily. "Now I eat dinner. That's as far as my mind seems capable of functioning."

"We're two of a kind," she admitted. "I'm not proud of my afternoon's work either. When will those beans be ready?"

"Not much longer. Once we get the rest of the meal organized, they should be warm."

In a surprisingly short time, they were sitting at opposite ends of the hammock, balancing plastic plates on their laps. The firelight at the end of the room provided a comfortable glow against the encroaching night. Rain continued to fall outside but the fire pit and the flickering candlelight made the hut snug against the storm. Fortunately the strong wind had dropped so the moisture-laden gusts which blew through the doorway at uncomfortable intervals had disappeared as well.

Their dinner menu tasted surprisingly good and, at the moment, water was heating in the emptied bean can for "after-dinner coffee" as Chris termed it. He had brought out two individual packets of coffee from his shirt pocket a few minutes before. "Left over from the airplane trip down," he explained. "I thought they might come in handy sometime. Especially since we've finished that in the jug."

"This is decaffeinated," Amanda was reading the label of the packet. "That's handy—but insomnia wasn't on my list of things to worry about." She looked up to find his eyes upon her and thought again that he had the most piercing glance she'd ever known.

"Exactly what," he wanted to know, "*is* on your list of things to worry about?"

She shrugged. "The sleeping arrangements for one thing. Since we're stuck here until morning, I realize we have to make the best of it. But even if we take turns on the floor it's going to be grim."

He got up to put his plate back in the picnic basket, saying over his shoulder, "If you want to spend part of the night on the floor ... go right ahead. Frankly I have no intention of it."

"I ... don't understand ..."

He turned to face her, an amused smile playing over his features. "That coy attitude isn't like you, Amanda. What's wrong with the hammock?"

"Not a thing." Her chin went up. "Unfortunately, we're not blessed with a plentiful supply."

"At least the one we have is good-sized ... and it can't be the first time two people have occupied a hammock in this country. Don't forget," he pointed out hatefully, "*you* were the one who wanted to come along on this jaunt. Don't tell me you're going to complain about a minor inconvenience."

His masculine arrogance acted like a spark to Amanda's temper. All her resolutions about being a good sport and "roughing it" evaporated like snow in a spring thaw. "I could write a book about the things I don't like on this trip," she began, "and you can stop laughing. This might all seem amusing to you—"

"Well, frankly, it's beginning to ..."

"I don't see anything the least bit funny about it," Amanda snarled. "The bugs are so thick that the gnats have to circle in a holding pattern while they wait for the mosquitos to take off from my arms and legs; my stomach is in a state of shock from the green pepper sauce on those beans and I feel as if I'd washed in a mud bath . . ." She surveyed her palms with disgust before continuing irritably. "But even those goodies pale into insignificance at the thought of spending the night in a hammock with you."

"Suit yourself but I don't know what you're worried about. Anybody who tried anything would either be a cockeyed optimist or need his head examined. A canoe looks like the Rock of Gibraltar by comparison."

"That wasn't what I had in mind at all," Amanda lied stoutly. "Obviously we wouldn't get any sleep huddled together . . ." Her voice trailed off as she noticed his preoccupied expression. "What's the matter?"

"I was just wondering . . . historians have never really known what happened to the Mayan race . . . why it eventually died out. Maybe sleeping in hammocks had something to do with it." He leaned back in the middle of theirs and proceeded to make himself comfortable. "Very interesting theory. Too bad you won't cooperate in testing it."

"Oh, honestly!" She stalked over to stand by the fire pit. "I hope you fall out on your head!"

"I'll be careful." He settled himself more firmly. "Go out and get some more wood if you want to keep that fire up. Incidentally, watch out if you sit down on that dirt floor. There are scorpions in this part of the country." He ignored her sudden indrawn breath and yawned. "Very nasty things if you come into contact with them. G'night, Amanda. I hope you manage to get some sleep. Shout if you need anything."

Amanda's face was a study as she watched him close his eyes and utter a contented sigh as he stretched out on the swaying hammock. Surely he couldn't be such a ... clod ... as to leave her on her own for the rest of the night just because she wasn't going to huddle in that miserable net with him. She took a determined step toward him and then paused uncertainly. She knew enough about Chris Jarrow by now to realize that he would no more change his mind than a piranha would ignore a passing goldfish at lunchtime. Not only that, if she started arguing, he would probably have her head just as unceremoniously.

She retreated to the fire pit and stood near the dying coals while she thought things over. The jeep was out; even if she could ignore the steady rain, she wasn't about to sit out in the underbrush while god knows how many jaguars strolled by. Of course, she could stand by the fire ... provided she went out in the darkness and got some more wood. She bit her lip as she considered it. Even gathering the wood in broad daylight didn't sound appealing. Conversely, she could sit down by the fire ... probably Chris was exaggerating about the scorpions ... but her back would be aching within a half hour. The only sensible thing would be to lean against the side of the hut ...

Her brooding glance went to the shadowed wall and surveyed the rough finish of sticks and mud plaster. All sorts of crawling things could be nesting in there and they wouldn't be averse to crawling down her neck if an opportunity presented itself ...

Later, she couldn't even remember walking from the fire pit to the hammock but her voice was firm as she leaned over it and prodded the recumbent form. "Chris ..." she waited until his eyelids rose slowly.

Deliberately, she was sure. Nevertheless, she went on. "I've changed my mind."

His only response was a noncommittal grunt.

"*Will* you move over or something," she said with exasperation. "How do I get in this thing? It's the first time I've ever shared a hammock."

"I should hope so." There was thinly veiled amusement in his tone as he rolled over on his side. "Maybe we'll both learn to love it. Come on ... lie down. Watch it, for god's sake ... you'll have us both on the ground," he warned as she put a cautious knee up. Then he pulled her down tight against his body in a way that brooked no argument.

Amanda struggled to get her nose out of his chest. "I'll smother at this rate," she complained. When there was no response, she wriggled gingerly, trying to put a discreet distance between them and then sighed because the slightest movement brought her smack up against his long, masculine frame. She gave up finally and found a comfortable spot on his shoulder for her head.

"That's the girl." His voice was close to her ear. "You know that old saying—'When faced with the inevitable ... relax and enjoy it.' "

"Humph." It was hard to express disdain when stretched at full length against a man. Especially when his arms were wrapped securely around her. "Good *night*, Mr. Jarrow."

This time, there was no disguising his rumble of laughter or the soft kiss that brushed her temples. "Good night, Miss Stewart. Don't forget to whistle if you want to turn over."

Chapter Seven

Amanda slept more soundly than she could possibly have imagined.

There were only one or two blurred intervals when her cramped position made her wake fitfully. Then she must have found a new spot on Chris's shoulder or nuzzled into his broad chest like a sleepy kitten because she couldn't remember anything else.

When she finally came wide-awake, pale rays of sunshine were invading the door of the hut and birds were twittering in the nearby trees. Amanda stretched luxuriously until her mind cleared and she sat up so suddenly that the hammock swayed and she had to cling to its sides. She stared at the empty netting around her, wondering how Chris had managed to leave without awakening her and where he'd gone. Then, outside, she heard the cough of the jeep engine and realized that he must be trying to get them on their way.

Her lips curved in a reluctant smile as she thought about the experience they'd shared. Far from being the ordeal she'd feared, the night had passed without any embarrassment at all. In fact, she found herself wishing that Chris weren't so conscientious in getting the jeep back in condition.

When she swung her feet to the floor of the hut, she noticed that their picnic gear had already been cleared away, leaving the interior free of any traces of the occupancy except for the hammock—and a man could hardly stuff *that* in the trunk with her body still in it.

From the steady throbbing of the jeep motor, it sounded as if Chris was trying to get it back on solid ground. Amanda concluded she'd better wash her face and be ready to go if he called. When she returned to the hut a short time later, he was emerging with the hammock under his arm and the jeep was back on the rocky track they'd followed the day before.

"I was just about to start hunting for you," Chris said tersely. "Why didn't you say where you were going?"

Amanda's cheerful "Good morning" stuck in her throat. "Why on earth should I?" she said instead. "You didn't tell me where *you* were going when you got up."

"You were sound asleep. I didn't want to send up any Roman candles until I found out whether I could dig the jeep out." He tossed the hammock into the box on the back with unnecessary vigor. "Now that you're here ... let's go. I've hung around this place long enough."

Amanda's eyes widened but she silently walked over to the jeep and slid onto the seat. She was no sooner settled than Chris put the car in gear and took off with a jolt that made her neck crack.

She opened her lips to protest and then closed them again after a glimpse of his stony profile. The bright sunlight spotlighted the lines of weariness around his eyes and the dark beginnings of a beard on his tight jaw. Water still glistened on his slicked-down hair but that was obviously the only amenity he'd enjoyed since getting up at dawn.

Amanda made another attempt at civility after they'd driven for a few minutes in complete silence. "If the air didn't feel so muggy, you'd never know there'd been a storm last night," she commented brightly. "Was it hard to dig out the wheels of the jeep or had the ground dried pretty well?"

He gave her the barest sideways glance. "Now what do you think?"

"Honestly, Chris, I'm not clairvoyant."

"That's obvious. Otherwise you'd have sense enough to stop babbling at this time of day."

His annoyed tone hurt her far more than she let on. "The thought *was* getting through to me. Sorry, I didn't realize you had such a rotten night."

He muttered something, then clamped down when he noted her pale features. His foot pressed down even harder on the accelerator and the jeep plowed through the still-dripping undergrowth like a thing possessed.

By the time they'd completed the journey back to the Hacienda, Amanda had managed to get her emotions under control. Womanlike, she had already run the gamut of despair, numbness, and finally pure annoyance at being ignored for the better part of the morning. When Chris finally turned in the drive and shut off the ignition, Amanda let out an unconcealed sigh of relief. She swung her legs over the side and stood up stiffly beside the jeep. "You don't mind if I hobble on up to my room?"

"Suit yourself." He bent over behind the seat to rummage on the floor, tossing his jacket impatiently aside in the process.

Amanda stood her ground, determined to quarrel even if it was only with the top of his head. "Any time you need somebody to go along with you on another trip . . ."

"I'll look in the yellow pages." He did glance up then, his eyes glinting with anger and something else harder to define. "Never mind, you can sleep all day and recover from your ordeal. Or sit on the side of the swimming pool and do your embroidery. Ives would be impressed with the feminine touch."

"I'd prefer seeing your manuscript since that's what I'm paid for."

"That's right . . . I'd forgotten you were the dedicated career woman." He slung his jacket over his shoulder and strolled around to her side of the jeep. "Good old Amanda, the only female I know with printer's ink in her veins."

"At least there's something still flowing in mine. You'd better see a doctor when you get home. The way you treat the opposite sex these days, I think some of your vital parts have withered away and you don't even know it."

He caught up with her by the steps and swung her around. "Complaining, are you? Well, there's a damned good way to find out. Let's run through it again."

Amanda twisted desperately to escape from his grip. "Will you let go of me! They have a million employees in this place; I'll bet every one of them is watching us."

He ignored her struggles, putting his other hand on her waist to draw her closer. "And enjoying the show. Relax, Amanda, I'm beginning to think that you need this more than I do . . ." He bent his head to kiss the side of her neck and then trailed his lips along her soft skin.

Amanda was agonizingly aware of his every movement and when his hands moved caressingly down her back, her body quivered in response.

Then all her resistance collapsed; her arms went

around his neck as she closed her eyes and her lips blindly sought his. Chris was right! This was what she wanted all along except she hadn't dared admit it. Breathlessly she waited for the moment when his lips would come down to cover hers.

Unfortunately the moment didn't come.

Instead she felt his hands tighten on her waistline so forcefully that she gasped before he abruptly pushed her away. She opened her eyes to see him at arm's length, still breathing hard as he stared down at her. Then he turned her around and she felt a smart cuff on her derriere as he urged her up the steps.

"After this, my girl, don't start something unless you're prepared to see it through." His eyes were starting to glint with laughter. "And your sense of timing is terrible—almost as bad as your driving." Before she could reply, he had swung on up the steps ahead of her to greet a figure standing in the shaded entrance. "Constancia! I hope you've got somebody cooking breakfast for us. We're hungry enough to eat our way through the menu."

"If that isn't just like a man!" The Mexican woman made her voice severe but a smile trembled on her lips. "You don't deserve any consideration at all, Christopher. We were worried sick when you didn't show up last night. I thought the nightmare was starting all over again."

She didn't look as if she'd lost a minute's sleep, Amanda thought dully as she continued toward them. At the same time, she was wondering if Chris changed his mind because he'd seen Constancia's gorgeous caftaned figure observing them or simply because he'd been testing her reactions all along. If the latter were true—now he had no doubts as to what her feelings were. No doubts at all.

"Amanda looks as if you'd been beating her," Constancia observed keenly. "Really, Chris, you should take more care of your betrothed."

"It wasn't his fault." Amanda paused in the archway beside them. "I got the jeep stuck yesterday. We had to wait until the rain stopped this morning before Chris could get it back on the road."

"Oh, my dear . . ."

Chris cut Constancia short. "It could have happened to anybody. Actually we managed very well—other than being a little short on sleep. And hot water," he added, rubbing his rough chin.

Amanda stared resentfully at his firm profile. His unruffled tone showed that he wasn't suffering any pangs of frustration or even annoyance. The bad temper he'd exhibited on their drive back had evaporated like the storm of the night before. One sight of Constancia had worked the miracle.

"Do you suppose Pablo could empty the jeep for us," Chris was asking the other woman. "I don't like to hang around doing it now."

"Yes, of course. If I can run him to earth." Constancia's honeyed tone turned acid. "He spends all his time with that dog of yours."

"How is Junior?" Amanda asked with one foot on the stairs.

"Well, there's certainly nothing wrong with his appetite. You'd think he hadn't eaten for weeks. Honestly, Chris," Constancia turned with a plaintive gesture, "that creature is a terrible nuisance."

"I know, *chica*," he bent to her attentively, "and you're wonderful to bend the rules for us. I can't tell you how much I appreciate it."

Amanda didn't wait to hear any more. She couldn't stand it, she decided, not on an empty stomach after a long night. To think she'd once believed

Chris was shy and uncertain with the female sex! "If you'll excuse me," she murmured.

"Where are you going?" Chris's sharp tone caught her halfway up the stairs.

"Really, Chris . . ." Constancia reproved. "Look at the poor thing! Isn't it obvious?"

That time Amanda didn't linger. Hitting one's hostess over the head didn't rank as justifiable homicide even in Mexico. Besides, if she got within arm's length of them she might have two murders on her hands. Instead, she sighed and followed the coward's way by scurrying up the stairs.

It took a long, leisurely bath and shampoo before Amanda felt capable of facing the competition again. Later, as she left her room to go back down, she had changed to a cool violet linen with a pleated skirt that was worth every penny she paid for it.

Unfortunately when she entered the dining room, she found that the only person to impress was a teen-aged waiter coming through the kitchen door.

He grinned admiringly and pulled out a chair for her. " *'Dias, Senorita,* you like breakfast now?"

"Very much." Amanda made herself unfold her napkin before looking around the room. "Where is everyone?"

He looked around, apparently hoping to find a customer crouched under a table for her. Then he shrugged and said, "The other gentleman—he eats early."

"Senor Jarrow, too?" Amanda kept her voice casual.

"*Yo no sé.* Maybe . . . in the room." He put a menu in her hands. "This morning . . . fresh papaya."

Amanda forced herself to concentrate on matters at hand, but when breakfast was over, she wandered listlessly out to the pool, thinking that it didn't help to be in a tropical paradise when there wasn't any loved one to share it. Guaca, the parrot, was concerned with the seed cup on his iron perch and only gave her a passing glance when she moved past him on the path. From the kitchen wing came the sound of chattering voices as the cooks made preparations for lunch but the hacienda registration desk was deserted and the gift shop door securely locked.

Amanda was about to settle for a rattan chair in the cool air of the foyer when a muffled bark came from the drive beyond. She hurried through the gate and found Pablo trying to coax Junior into the back of a Hacienda station wagon.

The big black dog paused as he caught sight of Amanda; one front paw lifted uncertainly.

Amanda paused, too, amazed at the difference one day's care had made in the dog's appearance; his rough coat had lost every snarl and now gleamed in the sunlight. Access to the Hacienda refrigerator had helped in the transformation as well. Junior's sides still had a concave look but his ribs no longer protruded like thin barrel staves.

"Junior ... you're positively handsome," she told him in admiration.

The sound of Amanda's voice was the only reassurance Junior needed. In a flash, he had pulled away from Pablo's side and was charging happily toward her. Amanda braced herself for a damp and ecstatic welcome.

Finally she was able to quiet him enough to lead him back to Pablo, saying, "You've done a wonderful job! I wouldn't have recognized him as the same dog."

Pablo beamed as he retrieved Junior's leash. "He's fine, I think, *senorita* ... except his paw. It doesn't improve. Today when I pick up the supplies at Playa Carmen, I thought I'd take him to a friend of mine. A kind of ... a *veterinario* ... you understand?"

She nodded. "That's a fine idea. He does seem to still favor that front leg. There could be an injury to the bone, I suppose. Poor baby ..." She knelt to caress the rough head and got a tongue in the face as Junior approved her attention.

"Would you like to come along, *senorita?* I pass through Can Cun on the way," Pablo said. "The government expects it to be as famous as Acapulco soon. And if there's time, we could drive on and see the ruins at Tulum ... unless you have something else planned."

"It sounds wonderful and I don't have a thing to do. If you'll just wait a minute until I get my purse and sunglasses, I'd love to go."

His smile broadened. "Don't hurry. Junior and I—we'll wait in the car."

Their trip through the lush countryside to the coast was made in happier spirits than the ride Amanda had shared with Chris earlier in the day.

Junior was so delighted to be included that he had trouble deciding whether he should stick his nose out the open window or wash Amanda's left ear so he compromised by doing both.

When commanded sternly—both in Spanish and English—to "Sit down and behave," he merely wagged his tail harder. "It's obedience school for you later on." Amanda informed him several miles beyond when he'd nearly fallen out the window barking as they passed a man on a motor scooter.

Aside from that near-catastrophe, a fine time was had by all. Pablo told how the natives made a favorite drink called *pozole* by diluting cornmeal with water and honey and later he pointed out gray chicle trees whose trunks were scarred with cuts that looked like surgical incisions. When Amanda casually switched the subject to Mayan customs and the Sacrificial Maidens, his pleasant face sobered.

"Always the Americans who come to the Hacienda want to talk about the maidens or the *cenote sagrado*. The Sacred Well at Chichen has thousands of tourists each year and I don't understand why." His wrinkled features were somber. "The Mayas weren't the only people who believed in human sacrifices. And remember, their acts were not done in anger. The victims were sent to carry petitions to the gods of rain and they were finely dressed and adorned with gold and jade to prove worthy messengers. You should ask Senorita Constancia to show you the copies of early Mayan jewelry which we make at the Hacienda. Both she and Don Miguel have taught our workers to duplicate the old pieces. Some of the finest designs come from the tomb of a king-priest at Palenque uncovered a few years ago."

Amanda pulled one of Junior's ears as the big dog rested his head on her shoulder. "I'm surprised to hear so much about jade here in Yucatán. I always associate it with strictly Oriental things."

Pablo gave her a droll look. "If you observe the carved faces on our temples, and the statues found at Jaina, they have a Mongolian cast as well ... even today, we are different from the rest of the Mexican people. We have the darker skin, straight black hair, and almond-shaped eyes. An Oriental look, you'd say. We're proud of it."

"With good reason," Amanda agreed. She gave Junior a sideways glance. "Too bad *you* couldn't have done better in the way of ancestors."

"Happily, dogs have the sense not to worry about such things," Pablo said.

She nodded. "I'll have to see the jade pieces in the Hacienda gift shop."

"They're very nice—especially the earrings in the shape of flowers or the necklace that looks like pumpkin seeds." He paused before adding somberly, "The stones have more than beauty."

"Oh?"

"The English word 'jade' comes from the Spanish '*ijada.*' *Piedra de ijada.* We translate it to Colic stone. It means a cure for disorders of all internal things"— he gestured toward his abdomen—"and it prolongs life by keeping you from getting fatigued. If taken just before death . . . it even preserves the body."

Amanda stared at his profile to see if he was serious and cleared her throat uneasily when she found he was.

"You doubt me, *senorita?*" He seemed amused. "Don't forget, the Mayas have tested such things all through their history."

"Oh, I don't doubt that . . ." She searched for a handkerchief to wipe her ear after another effusive salute from Junior. "I was just thinking that if you were already on the brink of death, a hefty dose of jade would certainly push you over. Frankly, I'd rather have something else for my last supper."

Pablo grinned good-naturedly. "Like our *Pollo Pibil* or *Torta del Cielo.*"

"They sound terrific. What are they?"

"The first is a chicken flavored with special Maya spices which we bake in a banana leaf. *Torta del Cielo* means Heavenly Cake; it's a festive almond torte that our women make for weddings." He bestowed a kindly look. "You must ask the cooks at the

Hacienda for them. There's also a special way of roasting venison . . ."

"Nope. You've lost me there. I'll stop with the chicken." She frowned slightly as she noticed a newly completed complex of huts on either side of the road. "What's all this?"

Pablo slowed the station wagon behind a heavily loaded dump truck which had swung in ahead of them. To the left, road graders were raising a haze of dust as they worked on a tract of land with partially constructed buildings set in a ring of palm trees.

"This," replied Pablo proudly, "is Can Cun. Some tourists call it the Caribbean Acapulco. Eventually we hope to have a million visitors a year."

By this time, they were in the thick of the new development with heavy construction equipment and laborers hard at work all around them. A few blocks to the left of the road, Amanda could see a dazzling expanse of white sand beach.

"Fifteen miles of it," Pablo boasted in her ear. "Once this was an island—now it's a peninsula and the largest resort-construction project in the hemisphere. Imagine, *senorita,* it is costing almost eighty million dollars!"

"It's amazing," Amanda murmured, dazed by such manna in the wilderness. "Is this where your friend lives? The one who's going to look at Junior's paw."

Pablo shook his head and accelerated as the traffic thinned. "No, *senorita.* Can Cun is for tourists only. My friends lives in Playa Carmen—a few more miles down the road. That is where I pick up our supplies, as well."

"Will you be very long?"

"I don't think so. There are some small restaurants overlooking the beach and the pier, where you can wait for me. Usually there are people waiting to take the ferry to Cozumel so there is always something going on."

"It sounds fine. Don't worry about me." She settled back in the seat again as they passed Can Cun's airport and were back almost immediately in scrub undergrowth. "I didn't know there was a ferry over to Cozumel—that's the famous island resort, isn't it?"

"One of the best places in the world for scuba diving," Pablo said, starting to sound like a tour guide. "And almost as famous for its sport fishing. Men catch sailfish morning and night in the waters off the coast. Senor Ives was asking about it yesterday."

"I didn't think he'd be able to resist those fishing rods of his very long," Amanda murmured. "Is that where he's gone?"

"I don't know for sure. His car was missing this morning, but he must have told Senorita Melgar of his plans."

A pleasant silence enfolded them for the rest of the drive down the coastline on the winding two-lane roadway. Even Junior was content to lie on the back seat with his nose between his paws and his eyes half-closed. The noontime sun was almost directly overhead when Pablo turned off the road onto a sandy track which led to the beach and some sprawling clusters of buildings.

It was evident immediately that Playa Carmen bore little resemblance to the planned magnificence of Can Cun. There were only a few tiny restaurants, a general store with a leaning front porch and a long concrete pier jutting into the choppy blue waters of the Caribbean. Several power cruisers were berthed alongside it and knots of curiosity-seekers wandered along the quay staring down at them.

"The ferry berths at the end of the pier," Pablo told her as he pulled carefully onto the shoulder of the road, avoiding the white sand beyond. "There is a good store farther down the beach if you want to buy something."

Amanda slipped on her sunglasses and prepared to get out of the car as soon as he stopped. "I'll probably just shop around. When will you pick me up?"

"An hour—*mas o menos, senorita.* If I have trouble finding my friend—it will take a little longer." He put a restraining hand on Junior's collar when the big dog surged to his feet and would have followed Amanda.

She nodded and opened the door carefully. "That's fine. I'll be ready whenever you are. Probably in one of those places having coffee."

"*Bien. Hasta la vista,*" Pablo leaned over to secure the door behind her and gave her a cheerful wave before reversing onto the road.

Amanda waved in return. She smiled ruefully as she heard Junior's howl of frustration and saw his anxious head at the rear window before the car disappeared around a corner. Poor Junior—life was just one disappointment after another for him.

She decided to stroll along the pier before walking to the gift shop farther down the beach. The breeze coming from the water helped to temper the blazing noontime sun and the broad walkway was more inviting than the tiny crowded restaurants which reeked of red peppers and beer. A little way down the pier she paused beside a tiny cart with a grill which advertised *Hamburguesa* and *Leche Malteada.* Since there was no apparent refrigeration, she was wondering how they managed to make malted milks without ice cream. When the young vendor grinned at her, she prudently indicated a warm bottle of lemonade and walked over to the pier railing to drink it.

A sudden surge of activity at the end of the pier

signaled the docking of the pocket-sized ferry from Cozumel and she saw a crowd of passengers start across the narrow gangway to the dock. The scattered chairs amidships and the luggage piled haphazardly on the stern showed that Coast Guard regulations weren't observed by the crew. As the passengers kept emerging from the lower deck, Amanda could only think of clowns emerging from a tiny Volkswagen in the center ring of a circus. She took another look at the turbulent waters of the Caribbean and gave silent thanks that she wasn't destined for a trip to Cozumel.

Thoughtfully she swallowed some more lemonade and wandered over to the other side of the pier to gaze down on the power cruisers bobbing from the pilings. Only a sleeping deckhand was in view on the boat closest to her but there was a flurry of activity on the one beyond. It was a modern blue-and-white cruiser with all the latest navigational aids, including two radar installations on the flying bridge. Two men were emerging from the main cabin as she watched. The first paused to oversee a hefty crew member as he transferred some scuba tanks to the stern of the boat. He was lifting them carefully, eventually positioning them so there would be no shifting once they were underway. Once he had finished, Amanda glanced casually back to the others before she turned away. As she identified Kent Ives's dark head, she stopped in her tracks as if she had been stoned. His startled glance and the way he moved deliberately to the stern of the boat away from her line of vision made it evident that he had recognized her as well and was determined not to show it. She frowned and stood on tiptoe, trying to keep him in sight. There was a hurried conversation with the man beside him, a final nod at the crewman, and then Kent had moved onto the boat behind him which had access to stairs leading up to the pier.

Amanda started to follow him before a hail from the food vendor made her realize she was carrying off his lemonade bottle. She grimaced with frustration and hurried to put it in his outstretched hand before turning back to catch Kent's attention. By then she discovered that he had disappeared in the melee of debarking passengers and others who, laden with baggage, were intent on boarding the ferry for a return trip to Cozumel.

Amanda found herself on the edge of the quay again trying to peer through the bobbing heads when she discovered that she was alongside the stern of the big blue-and-white cruiser. By now, the captain was talking to his crewman and testing the lashings of the scuba tanks himself. He was a deeply tanned individual dressed in white slacks and a knit sport shirt which clung to his slight but muscular form. Amanda's glance lingered on his sharp features and smooth dark hair as she tried to remember where she'd seen him.

His eyebrows drew together when he looked up to meet her intent stare. Then, she saw him wheel and mutter something to his crewman which made the other glower up at her, as well. The ferocity of their expressions made Amanda take an instinctive step backward. While she was still trying to get up her courage to ask them where to find Kent, she saw another crewman emerge from the cabin and hurry forward to loosen the bow line. At the same time, the captain went lithely up a side ladder to the flying bridge and started the powerful engines.

"Hey—wait a minute, will you?" It was doubtful that Amanda's vexed hail even reached the man's ears but he gave her another scowling glance as he waited for the stern line to be freed. Amanda's lips parted with amazement when his profile suddenly triggered her memory. It was Miguel Melgar—she was sure of it! But what was Constancia's brother doing aboard a luxury power cruiser at Playa Carmen when he was supposed to be in Guadalajara?

There was a subdued surge of noise from the hull below as the figure on the flying bridge briskly maneuvered the controls of the powerful twin screws. Then the gap of water alongside the cruiser widened as it parted from the mooring and headed for the open sea under full throttle.

"Damnation!" she murmured angrily, watching the cruiser slip neatly away. Certainly she hadn't expected to receive a royal reception from Miguel Melgar but neither had she expected outright hostility.

A blast erupted from the funnel of the Cozumel ferry as it announced its imminent sailing and two stragglers on the dock behind her broke into a run to get on board. Amanda ran a distraught hand through her hair as she moved out of their way. What should she do now, she wondered. Go back to a café and wait for Pablo or search the beach for Kent to find out why he had cut her dead?

An angry commotion on the fishing boat which had been anchored next to the Melgar cruiser drew Amanda's attention over the side of the pier again. Even as she watched, she saw the burly crewman who had loaded the scuba tanks shake off the restraining hand of another crewman as he started up the stairs to the pier. The hot flow of Spanish which they exchanged was a mystery to Amanda but there was no doubt that she figured in it. Both men glanced up at her, one with a worried frown, the other angry at being delayed. Seeing her attention upon them, the latter snapped an order to the other and bounded up the steps to the pier.

Amanda pulled back from the railing and stood in the middle of the concrete walk, wondering what to do next. Where before the pier had been crowded with ferry passengers, she now found herself alone on the span other than for the vendor by the lunch wagon who was busily replenishing his pop supply. Even as her startled gaze swept the walkway, she saw the crewman arrive at the top of the stairs and start toward her, effectively cutting off her access to the beach.

"*Mujer!*" He saw her startled expression and grinned lewdly. "*Si, Mujer . . . ven aqui.*" His rude gesture gave Amanda all the translation she needed. Without stopping to reason or argue, she turned and started running toward the end of the pier where a deckhand was shoving the crude gangway aboard the ferry.

"Wait!" Amanda shrieked at him breathlessly as she heard the other man's footsteps pounding on the concrete behind her. "Oh, please—wait for me!"

Her frantic call arrested the young man at the railing just after he had signaled the wheelhouse. Instinctively he reached out to grab Amanda as she plunged toward him, too terrified by then to be conscious of dangers from another side. The helmsman spun the wheel and struggled to keep the vessel in the berth for those vital last seconds as she leaped onto the deck. No sooner had the deckhand grasped her than the ferry slid out from the pier with a deafening blast of the whistle.

The man a few steps behind Amanda almost tried to follow her by leaping the gap; she could see the indecision on his face as she stood cowering in the deckhand's grasp. Then the warning blast made him visibly waver and his opportunity was lost.

A scorching stream of Spanish followed them across the widening gap of water. Amanda buried her head and the deckhand snarled something back that wasn't in any tourist phrase book. He confirmed it a minute later as he led her away from the rail. "That man's plenty mad, *senorita*. What did you do ... take all his money?"

"No. I think he's out of his mind."

The other looked back at the pier. "*Now* he is. Look at him shake his fist. It's a good thing this is my last trip today."

"I haven't even thanked you." Amanda put a shaking hand up to her cheek. "Thank god, you speak English."

"Sure ... we have lots of tourists visiting Cozumel. They go over for the diving. What about your bags?" He cast a professional eye at her. "And your ticket?"

"I don't have any. Can't I buy a ticket from you— round trip to Cozumel?" It was too bad they weren't going on to Miami, she thought. Or anyplace which would put a good-sized distance between her and that creature on the pier.

"I guess I can sell you one." The young man shrugged, losing interest now that the excitement was over. "Three dollars to go over. You'll have to buy a return ticket at the pier in Cozumel when the next ferry sails."

"Don't you turn around and come right back?"

He shook his head and started coiling some line by the railing. "This is an extra boat. We had some people on a tour who had to catch a bus at Playa Carmen. Better watch out, *senorita*," he warned as the vessel started rolling when it hit the offshore swells. "It was a rough crossing when we came over."

He guided her toward a steep stairway leading down to the main cabin below decks. "Maybe you can find a seat down there."

The air coming up the stairs blended an aroma of Mexican beer, green peppers, and perspiration, and it only took one whiff to make Amanda hastily draw back. "Please . . . can't I stay up here? I'd rather be out in the breeze."

He noted her colorless complexion and nodded understandingly. "How about sitting on that locker? Okay?" He kept a firm grip on her elbow to help her negotiate the now-heaving deck and pushed her onto a covered box by the stern railing.

Amanda managed to give him the money for her ticket before he left. "How long does it take to get to Cozumel?" she asked, a little surprised not to see the island looming in front of the bow already.

He shrugged again, balancing with difficulty on the shifting deck. "About two hours, more or less . . . depending on the weather." He waggled a hand casually. "You understand."

Amanda nodded, trying not to show the sudden sinking feeling that his announcement gave her. Her eyes wandered over the spartan outlines of the ferry and widened as she saw the size of the waves splashing over the side. She had two hours of sitting in the icy spray and hoping that they'd arrive in one piece!

She clung to the railing beside her, wondering if it wouldn't have been better to have faced up to the pursuer on the pier, after all. Then she shook her head wearily. As foolhardy as her plunge onto the ferry had been, she was convinced that she would have been in far greater danger from the crewman off the Melgar cruiser.

But why had Miguel Melgar issued the orders and why had Kent Ives deliberately avoided her? If only she'd stayed with Pablo and Junior—she'd never gotten in this trouble in the first place. She chewed on the edge of her lower lip nervously. Now what would Pablo do when he came to retrieve her and found her missing? Probably break all speed limits getting back to Chris to announce her disappearance. Then all hell would break loose!

Amanda closed her eyes and rested her head against the railing—too tired to cope any longer. The miserable ferry might just as well go to the bottom of the Caribbean, she decided forlornly. It would save her a lot of explaining later on.

Chapter Eight

During that interminable crossing, Amanda was able to console herself with one thing; at least she'd had sense enough to stay out on the open deck.

As the waves got higher and the currents buffeted the sides of the peapod ferry, more and more passengers reeled up from the lower cabin to seek the solace of the rail. When the flat outline of Cozumel appeared on the horizon in the middle of the afternoon, Amanda had been joined by at least a dozen unhappy souls who were equally delighted to see the end of the crossing.

Amanda had avoided being actually seasick but she was wishing heartily that she'd stuffed some traveler's checks in her purse so she could return to the mainland by plane instead of the rough-riding ferry. Despite that, she decided that she wouldn't call Chris from Cozumel to ask for help.

"One thing at a time," she murmured to herself, determined not to give in to self-pity. "You got yourself into this mess—you can jolly well get yourself out!"

Whether the deckhand who'd helped her aboard was alarmed to see her muttering to herself, or whether he was concerned that she might decide to debark as dangerously as she'd come aboard, would never be known. At any rate, he wandered back to give her an encouraging smile as the engines slowed by the Cozumel pier.

"Going to try some diving while you're here?" he asked companionably.

"Diving?" For a minute, Amanda couldn't think what he meant. Then she shook her head. "Oh, no, I don't know anything about it. Besides, I don't have any equipment."

"That's no problem. At Cozumel they rent everything in the dive shops. Any kind of gear ... tanks ... even boats. This year they've only lost two divers but they've had two hundred wounded on motorcycles."

"I wasn't planning on renting one of those either." She followed him over as he unhooked a chain at the end of the gangway. "What else can you do on Cozumel until the next ferry comes?"

He scratched his head as he thought about it. "I'd buy some *cerveza* and watch the people, but that's no good for a woman alone. Or you could take a horse cart to see the sights—except they're expensive."

Amanda thought of her thin wallet and the price of a return ferry ticket. "Never mind, I can buy a cup of coffee and watch the people. That's cheaper still."

He snapped his fingers. "*Ay, senorita*—I know the answer. Take a glass-bottomed boat. They cruise the reefs in front of the big hotels. Find one owned by Ernesto ... he's a friend of mine. That way it won't cost so much."

"Thanks. I'll keep it in mind." After his kindness, Amanda couldn't say that the last thing she wanted to do was to set foot on another boat. Even the thought of it made her stomach rumble warningly.

When she finally crossed the gangway and saw the main street of Cozumel, she was almost overwhelmed by the postcard beauty of the island resort. The boulevard was alive with color; a row of flame trees drew attention with their brilliant foliage while, at their base, multihued hibiscus and bougainvillea vied for blooming space. Tall coco palms dotted the shoreline in front of magnificent resort hotels which stretched down the island on either side of the business areas. But most spectacular of all were the white sand beaches, vibrant against the emerald and azure tones of the tropical waters.

Amanda's journey past the few blocks of stores and specialty shops confirmed another thing she'd heard; Cozumel was definitely the mecca for scuba divers. She slowed to let two bearded college types argue its merits on the sidewalk in front of her.

"I tell you, man, you can't beat it," one of them was saying. "I was down yesterday. Imagine! Almost three-hundred-foot visibility here when you're lucky to have thirty in California."

"Yeah, I know. I'm going for the black coral on my next try," the other said happily. "I'm trying for a place on the boat tomorrow. Two-hundred-foot depth—and you get all you want."

Amanda's steps lagged in the afternoon heat and she pushed her hair back from her face. Just then she would have happily traded two hundred feet of water for six inches in a wading pool. Since that wasn't possible, the best thing she could do was to buy her ferry ticket and then find a shaded restaurant to wait for the next sailing.

The ticket window on the pier was closed but a sign indicated the final ferry back to the mainland sailed at seven o'clock ... an hour later than she'd thought. Despondently, she walked back to a tiny restaurant with some sidewalk tables in sight of the pier. At least she could make sure that she didn't miss the boat.

It was almost a half hour later when she looked up from a Mexican picture magazine left by another customer to see the big blue-and-white power cruiser rapidly coming in to a mooring close by the ferry landing. It took only a moment to identify the broad shoulders of the crewman she'd managed to elude in Playa Carmen as he stood waiting to leap ashore and secure the bow line.

Amanda managed to find some pesos in her purse and leave them on the table next to her unfinished drink before she hurried around the block toward a taxi rank she'd seen earlier.

A waiting cabdriver merely nodded when she pointed down the boulevard. When he asked her destination after a few blocks, she was confused for a minute and then remembered a hotel she'd seen advertised in a shop window. They drew up in the impressive curved drive a few minutes later and she was pleased to note it was a good distance from the shopping center.

She smiled apologetically at the bellman who came out for her luggage and followed her back, empty-handed, into the spacious lobby. She evaded the inquisitive glance of the clerk at the reception desk and strolled over to a couch, trying to look as if she were waiting to meet a guest in the lobby. Certainly she was inadequately dressed for the opulent surroundings of the big room; even the floor was exotic, comprised of stark white marble squares under the groupings of contemporary black leather chairs and couches. At the far side of the room, a curving stairway of white marble slabs without any visible means of support rose majestically to balcony level. On the ocean side, floor-to-ceiling windows looked out onto the palm-shrouded beach. Every inch of the white sand had been carefully raked and the trunk of each palm had been whitewashed to shoulder level. Close by, a kidney-shaped pool was surrounded by colorful lounges to provide for guests who found the Caribbean too primitive for their tastes.

Amanda unobtrusively smoothed some of the wrinkles from her skirt as she sat on the edge of a couch and tried to remember how much money she had left. From the looks of the hotel, it certainly wouldn't be enough to pay for dinner. She glanced around again and saw the man at the reception desk holding a muted conversation with the bellman who had followed her in. Their suspicious appraisal made her cheeks flame with anger. If only she'd thought to bring enough money!

She made a production out of looking at her watch and then got up to walk over to a side door which led out to a path marked "Beach." As soon as she left the main building, however, she changed her pace. One way or another, she'd have to waste time until the ferry departure. By then, possibly the Melgar cruiser would have left the pier or there'd be nobody on deck to see her boarding the ferry back to the mainland.

Occupied with her thoughts, she moved slowly along the flagstone walk. The guest wings of the hotel stretched along the beachfront behind her, the native stone-and-wood construction blending easily into the landscape. Each room had a private lanai so guests could enjoy a surf view from their balconies.

Amanda lowered her eyes to the ground as she scuffed through the sand, knowing she was receiving curious stares from sparsely clad guests who generally wore more suntan lotion than anything else. In turn, she felt uncomfortably overdressed in pumps, nylons, and her rumpled linen dress. It was no wonder that the desk clerk had eyed her so dubiously.

She watched a couple dash into the gentle surf and heard the sound of their laughter before she turned to wander even farther up the beach. Once she stopped to investigate an outcropping of rock and knelt, fascinated, watching schools of tiny fish swim through its fissures. The wonderful clarity of the water made it seem like a giant salt aquarium, and Amanda stayed until two youngsters in swimming trunks arrived with plastic bags to try their luck at capturing some marine specimens.

A short jetty marked the end of the hotel's property and Amanda strolled out on it to admire a small canopied boat of Boston whaler type.

"Like to take a ride, lady?"

Amanda turned, startled, to find a grinning teenager behind her. His tanned body was clad only in a pair of cut-off denims but he gestured authoritatively toward the bobbing craft. "Everybody who comes to Cozumel should ride in a glass-bottom boat."

"Your name wouldn't be Ernesto, would it?" she asked hopefully. As his grin widened, she went on. "The man on the ferry recommended you."

His shoulders went back. "For friends . . . I have a special price. Besides," he added ruefully, "business is lousy today. How long a trip do you want?"

"Just until the ferry leaves at seven. Perhaps you could take me back to the ferry landing . . . it would save me a taxi fare. How much would it all cost?"

He glanced at his watch. "Four dollars be okay? That's half my usual rate."

She nodded hesitantly. If she didn't spend any money on food until she got back to the mainland, her budget would just about stretch that far. And once she arrived at Playa Carmen, she could arrange to pay at the Hacienda for the rest of her trip.

"Is it okay, *senorita?*" For all his show of nonchalance, there was an undercurrent of anxiety in Ernesto's voice. Business must have been very bad indeed.

"It'll be fine, thanks." She followed him out to the end of the pier and stared down at the bobbing craft in some dismay. "How do I get down to it?"

"I'll help you. *Momento, por favor.*" Ernesto was over the edge and into his boat in an instant. In a few deft motions he had snubbed up the line holding it to the pier and was extending two strong arms. "Sit on the edge of the dock, *senorita* ... then just lean forward. I'll catch you."

Surprisingly, it was as easy as that. Once aboard, Amanda grasped an iron support for the striped sun canopy while Ernesto dusted off a seat on one side and then ushered her carefully into it. It was providential that he took care of such details, because, by then, all of Amanda's attention was on the big glass rectangle in the bottom of the craft and the wonderful creatures swimming in the clear water beneath.

"It's fantastic," she murmured. "Absolutely fantastic!" For the first time, all her troubles were pushed to the back of her mind as she hung over the glass bottom. "What's that big one down by the piece of coral?"

Ernesto grinned with pleasure as he sat down and started the outboard. "A grouper, *senorita.* But wait till we get out on the reefs ... then you'll see the really big ones!"

With a roar of the motor, he nimbly maneuvered the craft away from the pier and headed for open water at a speed which made Amanda hastily hang on. She opened her mouth to protest as they cut across the wake of a power cruiser and then closed it again. From Ernesto's rapt expression, he had done this many times before and wouldn't welcome any back-seat driving from his passenger. At least he wasn't reading a comic book at the same time, like the man in the wheelhouse of the Cozumel ferry when the waves were doing their worst.

Suddenly the roar of the engine slackened and Ernesto leaned forward to peer through the glass bottom himself. "There's the reef," he announced matter-of-factly. "This is the best place to watch."

Amanda couldn't dispute his knowledge. For the next hour and a half, he let the boat bob on the waves while they both stared at the never-ending stage below them. There were schools of fish in every size, some brightly colored against the banks of coral, others looking like quicksilver against the white background. The small ones made way for the larger ones that came along . . . another slow-moving grouper whose size made Amanda gasp and then an evil-looking shark who circled in the depths below them, cleaving the water so purposefully that when Amanda remembered the thin pane of glass separating them from his wicked jaws, she could only shudder and hope he would move on.

As the time went by, Ernesto would let the boat drift until they moved too far over the swells for good reef viewing. Then he would start the motor and bring them back to his chosen spot.

Amanda wasn't conscious of the passing minutes, until she finally raised her head and discovered how dizzy she was. She shivered suddenly as the water heaved in another swell and then felt her stomach muscles protest when the tiny craft bobbed up in response before swooping down into the trough.

"Ernesto . . ." She had to swallow before she could

get his name out. "I think we'd better go ... right now!"

The misery in her voice brought his head up like a shot. Probably, she thought later, he'd heard those warning tones before ... from other passengers on rough and windy days.

Now even a glimpse down through the glass made her head reel and she leaned against the canopy support behind her, taking deep breaths of the salt breeze. She was not ... *not* ... going to be seasick, she told herself firmly.

Ernesto, probably with more practical motives in mind, told her the same thing. He hastily started the engine and spoke over its noisy sputter as they headed closer to shore. "Take it easy, *senorita*. We'll be where the water's calmer in a few minutes. Close your eyes. Sometimes that helps."

Amanda did as he directed but she couldn't clamp down on the thoughts that were racing through her head. If her stomach felt like this now, how would it ever survive two hours of tossing on the return ferry trip? She would like to have wept in sheer desperation but made herself sit quietly and try to ignore the motion.

When they finally approached the ferry pier, Ernesto slackened his speed to search for a mooring. Amanda looked around and then suddenly reached over to lower the canvas side canopy which protected passengers during really rough weather.

Ernesto turned to stare at her. "There is no need for that, *senorita*. We're almost at the ferry pier now."

"Please, Ernesto, just do as I ask and don't ask questions. Let your motor idle as if you were looking for a place to pull alongside."

He shot her an inquisitive glance but did as she

requested. "What am I supposed to be looking for, *senorita?*"

"A man ... a rough-looking crewman ... with shoulders as wide as that shark we saw on the reef. I think I saw him by that blue-and-white cruiser."

Ernesto's hand went up to shield his eyes from the reflection of the setting sun on the water. "I see the one you mean, *senorita*. Only he's not by the cruiser now."

Amanda allowed herself a moment of hope. "Where is he? Going to one of the bars, maybe?"

"No such luck, *senorita*. He's over by the gangway to the ferry. They've just lowered the chain to start loading." Ernesto's young face registered sympathy at her obvious despair. "Is he waiting for you, *senorita?*"

Amanda pressed farther back against the side curtain. "I'm afraid so. He doesn't look as if he's about to move, does he?"

Ernesto turned his craft in a lazy circle alongside the pier before pointing the bow toward open water again. "He's just lit a cigar and is leaning against the pier railing . . . watching people get on the ferry. What do we do now, *senorita?*"

"I wish I knew." Amanda saw Ernesto sneaking a look at his watch and realized that he probably was long overdue at home—plus being long overdue for dinner. The thought of food made her take another deep breath and let it out slowly. At least it wouldn't be hard for her to save money on her own dinner.

Ernesto was leaning forward anxiously. "The ferry's pulling out, *senorita* . . . and it's the last one until tomorrow morning. Maybe you'd better go back to the hotel. It's a very good hotel."

She nodded and hung onto her seat for support as

he gave her a relieved grin and applied full power to the motor. As the boat bounced over the top of the waves, Amanda told herself that there was a time to fight and a time to surrender. Feminine pride was all very well, but right now she was consigning hers to the sharks and barracudas. After she'd paid Ernesto and tipped him handsomely for his efforts, she would have just enough for a long distance call to the Hacienda. Even if Chris weren't there, Constancia surely could vouch for her with the Cozumel hotel management for an overnight stay.

If she couldn't ... Amanda frowned and rubbed her forehead ... that was an obstacle for the future and there was no point in worrying about it now. Not when she already had a list of problems demanding her immediate attention.

Ernesto throttled back on the motor and added one more. "There's a man waiting at the end of the hotel pier. No—maybe not"—he was squinting along the water—"he's walking back now. I guess he's not interested in us."

"Thank heavens for that!" Amanda stayed out of sight behind her canvas, wondering if she'd have to hire Ernesto to take her all the way to Tampa Bay. "It's not the same man who was at the ferry dock, is it?"

"How could he be, *senorita?*" Ernesto had no patience for feminine logic. "This man was a *turista* ... probably he will be back to hire me tomorrow. I have many friends who send me customers."

"And you deserve every one of them," she said as he cut the motor and moved forward to secure the bow line. She found her wallet and folded some bills carefully before inching her way to the stern where Ernesto was waiting for her. "I'll never forget this afternoon," she told him.

He looked troubled as he took the money and weighed it on his open palm. "This is more than we agreed, *senorita*. You might need it since you've missed the ferry . . ."

She folded his fingers over the currency and shook her head. "Honestly, I'll be fine. Will you give me a boost up on the pier, please?"

Ernesto nodded reluctantly and leaned over, lacing his fingers together. "Step in here—wait for the swell . . . now, *senorita* . . ." At the crest of the wave, he gave her a boost up the side of the rough piling, launching her precipitously onto the pier. "You okay, *senorita*?"

Still on her hands and knees, she leaned back over the edge to assure him. "Fine, thanks."

"That's good." Ernesto was staring past her shoulders. "Oh, oh. He's coming back, *senorita*."

Something in his voice made Amanda scramble to her feet. It only took a split second for her to recognize the tall figure in slacks and sport coat striding down to the pier toward her. Her face lit up like one who has seen the heavens open. "Chris!" she murmured incredulously. Then as he reached out for her, she said again, "Oh, Chris!" with such joy that Ernesto grinned and started securing his boat for the night. There was no doubt—his *"senorita"* was in good hands.

Chris tightened his arms about Amanda's trembling form as if he didn't know whether to shake her, spank her, or follow his instincts and do both. While he was making up his mind, he grasped a hank of hair to pull her nose out of his lapels and kissed her so forcefully that Ernesto's eyes widened in admiration.

When Amanda finally managed to draw back, she opened her mouth to protest but Chris simply put a hand on the back of her head and turned her face into his chest once again. "Now, where in the devil have you been all day?" he began in a dangerous level tone that boded ill for any defensive tactics.

"Well, it's a long story . . ."

"I'll bet. Do you realize I've spent the last five hours trying to catch up with you? If I finally hadn't found the taxi driver who brought you here, I'd have called in the police by now."

"Well, I didn't plan it this way."

"You didn't plan—period." He scowled down at her. "Incidentally, you look awful. I suppose you forgot to eat."

"Now there, you're wrong!"

Amanda was about to launch into a graphic description of why she didn't want to eat again . . . ever . . . when he said abruptly, "Not only that . . . I found you hadn't registered at the hotel. Damned if I can see why you had to go larking around in a glass-bottomed boat before even getting a place to sleep."

"Look, will you let me . . ."

"It's all right," he brushed her protest aside. "I was able to fix us up. They're used to eccentric Americans. The clerk didn't bat an eye when I said you'd come off without any luggage."

"You needn't make me sound like . . ."

". . . a stubborn, cockeyed idiot! Why not? That's what you are." Now that Amanda was securely in his arms, Chris felt a relief in anger. "Pablo comes back to the Hacienda wringing his hands after looking all over Playa Carmen for you . . ."

Her head came up. "Is Junior going to be all right?"

"Sure, fine." Chris scowled and reverted to his tirade, "Stop changing the subject. If Kent hadn't called and said you were on the Cozumel ferry dock, I'd still be scouring the beachfront over there. Damned if I can figure you out."

"You mean ... Kent didn't even explain?" She would have pulled away but his arms tightened across her back.

"There wasn't time. Besides, that's all I needed to hear." He looked around irritably. "Are you passionately attached to this pier?"

"Well, no ... but ..."

"Then let's get the hell out of here." He started marching her back down the jetty.

Amanda tried once again. "Honestly, Chris ... if you'd listen to me for a second ..."

He pulled to a stop. "Amanda ... do me a favor and stop arguing, will you?"

"I'd like to, but——"

He cut in again. "That's the trouble with women. I've always said so." There was a suspicious gleam of laughter in his eyes as he urged her up the sandy beach on the path leading to the hotel.

"What do you mean—the trouble with women?" Amanda finally asked in spite of herself.

"They never let a man get a word in edgeways, that's what." He patted her shoulder consolingly. "I'll have to admit though ... you've been better than most."

Chapter Nine

After that remark, Amanda should have held her ground and protested. Strenuously.

It wasn't as if she didn't have a sizable list of things to object to. First off, no woman in her right mind would have followed him across that elegant lobby looking as she did. One quick peek in an antique mirror confirmed that her hair was hanging limp against her neck from its second bout with salt spray, and the only charitable thing that could be said about her dress was that it still covered her.

She could only stand and stare when the desk clerk ignored such trivia, pressing a key in her hand and wishing them a pleasant stay. Both she and Senor Jarrow must call on the hotel management if they had the slightest problem.

"That'll be the day," Amanda muttered as Chris moved her toward the marble steps beyond the reception desk. "He looked at me as if I'd floated in with the tide before. What did you tell him when you registered?"

"Just that I wanted a pair of rooms." Chris turned down the marble corridor to their left, checking the room numbers on the way. Suddenly he stopped in front of an elaborately carved door. He plucked the key from her fingers and unlocked it, pushing it open. "This is yours, unless you object to the far-out color scheme."

When Amanda entered the tiled hallway she saw he was right about the decor. The bedroom was done in shades of orange and the colors were followed on an elaborate half-canopied bed, a deep shag rug, and the long draperies at the sliding doors leading to the room's balcony.

"My room's next door. Substitute purple for orange and we're a matched pair," Chris explained. "But the air-conditioning works . . ."

"And there's a gorgeous roof over our heads." Amanda sank onto the side of the king-sized bed and bounced gently on the springs. "A little while ago, I would have settled happily for that." She stopped suddenly in mid-bounce. "You *do* have some money, don't you? Right now, my assets consist of one American dollar, twenty-two Mexican pesos, and three green stamps."

"You wouldn't last long with that," he grinned. "Maybe one bottle of beer if you didn't tip the waiter."

"I had other plans."

"Like buying a Spanish phrase book that gave the word for 'Help!'?" Chris was lounging against the edge of the mirrored dressing table but there was nothing relaxed about his expression; his probing glance was taking in every detail of her pale, weary face. "Or had you finally decided to sink your pride?"

"Something like that." She was fiddling with the fringe on the bedspread rather than meet his eyes. "If you must know, the next item on my agenda was a long distance call to you."

"Well, hoist the flag. I never thought I'd see the day."

She grinned crookedly. "While you're raising that flag, make it a white one. You'll never believe what's happened to me today."

He got up and moved over to the door. "Let's stow the explanations for a while. I'll be back in a few minutes and you can tell me then."

She put up a hand to stop him. "Chris, will you *please* listen to me. I tell you, I've been scared out of my wits for hours. I didn't come over here because I had a sudden urge to see the scenery."

"I gathered that," his tone was as grim as the set of his jaw. "Or at least some of it. Kent did some talking. Why do you think I was so relieved to find you on that pier? Those New York editors would take a dim view if you turned up missing."

Amanda felt a twinge of unhappiness go through her at his words. The day's events had exhausted her but she wasn't so tired that she couldn't recognize his warning. Anything he'd done or said on the pier was merely reaction. If she chose to misinterpret it, that was strictly her affair.

She leaned over to plait the bedspread fringe with careful fingers. "You'll have to come up with a pretty good story. I know I can't—right now I feel as if I'd wandered into a nightmare with my eyes wide open."

"The damnable part is—it isn't over yet. Except for your part in it." His glance was honed as it flicked over her. "You're retiring while you're still in one piece. Right now."

"Is that an order?"

"You're a young woman of unusual perception too. I always said so. Now, lie back on that bed and rest. I'll lock the door behind me when I leave. Don't open it for anybody until I get back."

She followed his order reluctantly, propping the

pillows behind her. "What if somebody hollers 'fire'?"

"Go out on the balcony and wait for the hook and ladder. If the flames start licking your ankles, you have my permission to jump. You should survive an eight-foot drop to the beach. Any other questions?" Then as he caught the dangerous glint in her eye, he grinned and opened the door. "You can save *that* one until I get back."

Amanda smiled back at him before the door closed. She couldn't help herself. The mattress felt wonderful and while the humidity gave the bed linen a soggy quality, at least the air-conditioner made the room refreshingly cool.

Of course, she should be combing her hair and trying to look presentable. Or at least brushing the wrinkles from her dress. Even as she considered the futility of the latter ... her eyelids went down and she drifted off in a light sleep.

The next thing she heard was the sound of the door opening after a brief warning knock. She managed to push up on one elbow as Chris came back in the room carrying a leather vanity case.

"I'm glad to see you were sensible." His glance roamed over her. "You look a little better. Here ..." he thrust the case at her as she swung her feet to the floor and stood up. "I thought you could use a change of clothes and maybe a toothbrush."

Her eyes gleamed as she clutched the handle. "*Could* I?"

"If you want to go in the other room and change, I've arranged for the maid to press your dress. She's waiting outside." He shook his head impatiently as Amanda hesitated. "Just hand it out the door to me," he said, pushing her toward the bath. "Incidentally, I've ordered dinner in fifteen minutes so don't fall asleep in the tub."

"Right now, soap and hot water sound better than steak. It's going to take time for this transformation," she added around the crack of the door before the wrinkled dress was handed out to him.

"In that case, I'll give you twenty minutes. No more." He looked amused as she closed the door decisively in the middle of his ultimatum.

Amanda turned the bathroom taps on full force and then opened the vanity case to inspect the contents. She happily removed a travel kit containing a toothbrush and a stick of solid cologne but her attention was on a tissue-wrapped package which turned out to be hostess pajamas in turquoise silk shantung. They were severely tailored with a mandarin collar but underneath in another parcel was a full-flowing matching robe with a wonderful flaring skirt, a satin shawl collar, and obi sash. High-heeled slippers consisting of a few straps of turquoise leather rested at the bottom of the case.

Amanda abandoned her new finery reluctantly to set a new speed record with her bath and shampoo but when she finally finished donning the glamorous outfit, she felt strangely shy about appearing in it.

The sound of the hall door opening and a waiter's voice made her realize she couldn't linger much longer. She waited just long enough to run the stick cologne over the inside of her wrists and hear the door close again before poking her head out to make sure the coast was clear.

"I was about to send in the Marines," Chris told her from the center of the room where he was hovering over their dinner. As his glance went over her, a suspicion of a grin flickered on his features. "On second thought, I'm glad I didn't."

By then, she was used to his oblique compliments. Gravely she pirouetted before him. "It's gorgeous. Far too nice for just sleeping." Then as she saw an eyebrow go up, she added hastily. "Be sure and remember how much I owe you. I'll pay you when I get back to the Hacienda."

"I'll remember." He yanked out a chair for her. "Sit down, will you. The steak's getting cold and the beer's getting warm." As she came over, he added, "I thought we'd do better here than on the balcony. Dinner by candlelight may be romantic but it also attracts every moth for miles."

She was glad to follow the safe topic. "Besides, we had dinner by candlelight last night, so it's old hat."

"Uh-huh. Better try some of that melon." He pulled up a chair for himself and unfolded his napkin. "Thank god we won't have to fight the battle of the hammock again."

Amanda tried to look interested in the broiled steak on the plate before her while she digested his comment. It was evident that Chris hadn't harbored any sentimental feelings for the hours they'd spent together in the hut. While she was treasuring memories, he was happily exchanging it all for an innerspring mattress. She stabbed her fork into the meat so hard that juice spurted.

"I hope that steak's the way you like it." He was paying closer attention than she'd thought.

"Just right. Do you mind if I settle for coffee rather than beer? I need something to revive me after all that's happened."

"I'm not surprised." He reached for the silver pot in the middle of the table. "Do you feel like talking about it now or shall we wait until after dinner?"

She sat back in her chair and toyed with the handle of her coffee cup. "Actually I'd like to tell you—

maybe you can make sense out of it. Darned if I can."

While he listened, she described all that had happened since she'd left Pablo and the dog in Playa Carmen that morning. Her recital of her escape on the pier made Chris's eyebrows draw together in an ominous scowl which stayed on his face for the rest of her story.

When her voice finally trailed off, he put his elbows on the table and leaned forward to regard her intently. "You're sure that same crewman was on the ferry pier tonight? The one from the Melgar cruiser?"

"I'm positive." She started to take a sip of coffee and then put the cup back in the saucer without tasting it. "What has he got against me? For that matter, why should Constancia's brother be angry to find me by his boat in the first place? And why did Kent cut me absolutely dead when he saw me?"

"Damned if I know. He didn't go into details about Miguel and the cruiser ... just said that you were in Playa Carmen and that you needed me. Once I got there, I found a little guy selling things on the pier who remembered your dash to the ferry."

"But how did you get to the island so fast?"

"Took a plane from Can Cun ... we'll go back the same way in the morning except that we can land on a private strip near the Hacienda. Unless you're keen for another ferry ride."

Amanda shuddered visibly. "I'd rather try Huck Finn's raft than go near that thing again."

Chris smiled absently, his thoughts on something else. "I wonder if that crewman wanted to question you. It makes more sense than any other theory."

"I suppose you're right. But why? Unless there

was something suspicious about those scuba tanks they were loading . . . but they looked perfectly normal to me."

"Maybe Miguel thought you were somebody else."

"So he sent that man to find out?" She nodded as she considered it. "That could be it. But why isn't Miguel in Guadalajara as he's supposed to be?"

"There could be a thousand explanations for that. Maybe he changed his plans and didn't tell Constancia. After all, she's just his sister, not his keeper."

Amanda shot a derisive look across the table. "There's a masculine answer if I ever heard one."

He merely looked amused. "What did you expect? Besides, I think you've got the wrong end of the stick on this thing. The important question is why Kent was in such a hurry to leave the dock without recognizing you." Chris put his napkin on the table and stood up. "It's time I got to work."

"What are you going to do?"

"Try to go aboard that cruiser if it's still at the dock." He went on hurriedly when she opened her mouth to protest. "That's no problem. There are plenty of tourists who want to hire a dive boat."

"I suppose so. What about Kent?"

"That shouldn't be too hard either. José's brother . . . the fellow I talked to in Mérida . . . knows everything that's going on in this part of the country. I'll call him from here." He frowned. "That's better than trying to phone from the Hacienda."

"Maybe you'd better call Constancia, too. She's apt to wonder why we're both missing," Amanda said. "Especially after being gone last night."

His lips quirked as if she'd said something amusing but all he said was, "Constancia's a big girl now. She'd be a lot more amazed if I let my fiancée go wandering off to Cozumel alone."

"I . . . I forgot about that." Amanda's cheeks became pink. "Of course, she doesn't know that we didn't . . . that nothing has . . ." Her voice trailed off as she realized she was only making matters worse. Chris's carefully smothered smile showed that he enjoyed her confusion. For an instant, her fingers itched to throw the roll basket at him, but she managed to stand up without yielding to her impulse. "What would you like me to do?"

He came around the table beside her and gently rubbed a thumb across her delicate cheekbone. "Not what I'm going to tell you," he said. "Most couples who come here for a holiday finish the evening with a midnight swim. This water's so warm and smooth on your skin that it's unbelievable. The moonlight looks like platinum on the sand and there's an off-shore breeze to rustle the palm fronds overhead when you stroll down the deserted beach afterwards."

There was a telling silence when his words tapered off. Amanda stood like a small statue under his caressing hand, aware that her heart was thundering in her breast but unaware that her eyes reflected her wistful desires.

Chris chose to disregard her silent appeal. He took a deep breath and stepped back, letting his hand fall to his side as he said tersely, "You'd better go to bed. It's been a hell of a day." He walked over to check the lock on the balcony door. "Keep this closed. The air-conditioning will have to serve tonight. After I leave, put the chain on the door." He moved past the bed to the hallway. "I'll order breakfast for seven thirty. With any luck, we can take off for the Hacienda right after that."

Amanda pushed her own hands deep in the pockets of her robe to hide their trembling. "Is it all right if I brush my teeth?" she asked, trying to keep her voice as matter-of-fact as his.

One corner of his mouth went up slightly. "I have no objection . . . provided you don't linger over it."

"It must be nice for a man to have so many interests," she remarked conversationally, following him to the hall door. "Think of the job opportunities . . ."

He pulled up warily with his hand on the knob. "Such as?"

"Well, if you get tired of being a college professor or a writer, you can always try for a position as a dictator. Maybe a small South American country—they have more jobs open. The turnover, you know."

His eyes glinted but it was hard to see whether it was with laughter or annoyance. Aloud he said merely, "Remember . . . don't open the balcony door, don't leave the room, and don't forget to put the chain on this door once I've gone." He pulled it open, hesitating on the threshold. "And don't look at me like that, little one." His palm came up to cup her cheek briefly. "I don't like it one damned bit better than you do."

Chapter Ten

Things moved so rapidly the next morning that Amanda didn't have a chance to ask Chris about his night's activities until they left the hotel in a ramshackle taxi on their way to the Cozumel airport.

The old cab lurched along the shore road in a cloud of exhaust which would have had America's clean-air advocates wringing their hands. The driver kept one hand on his gear shift to discourage it from sliding into neutral while the engine emitted sporadic backfires sounding like a launching pad at Cape Canaveral.

After a particularly violent one, Amanda looked over to find Chris with a broad grin on his face. "Now what?" she asked.

"One ride in this and even an FBI man would surrender." He winced as they bounced briskly through a pothole without slackening speed. "I'll be damned, if I'd hit that thing, we'd still be sitting there."

"It's different when you have tread on your tires." She bit her lip suddenly. "I don't mind this carefree attitude when we're on the ground but if the pilot hands me a pair of goggles and asks me to wind the prop . . . I'm waiting for the next plane."

"I wonder if we'll even get to the airport," Chris said, frowning at his watch. "We're cutting it fine on the time as it is."

"Well, surely the pilot will wait. It's a charter plane, isn't it?"

"I'm not worried about that . . . I want to keep an appointment later on. After I deliver you to the Hacienda."

"Look here," she told him firmly, "I didn't mind being treated like the 'frail little woman' last night . . ."

"Not much, you didn't. You were just too tired to do anything about it." He was interrupted by a sudden sneeze on her part and scowled as she rooted in her purse for a handkerchief. "Not catching cold, are you?"

Amanda didn't like his tone. "Certainly not. I never catch cold." Her declaration was somewhat spoiled when she sneezed again, but she said, "It was the air-conditioning last night," and blew her nose. "I wish you'd stop changing the subject. What did you discover when you went back to the pier?"

"That the cruiser had pulled out earlier. Right after that last ferry to the mainland. You were right though—the boat belongs to the Melgars and Miguel was aboard. He's well known here in Cozumel. Apparently he spends a lot of time diving in these waters."

"That could account for the scuba tanks. But I still don't see why he was so upset when I appeared."

"It's not strange when you hear the rest of it—the really important part." He hesitated and glanced toward their driver but the man was humming to himself, apparently oblivious to everything except the road ahead. Another backfire shook the car and Chris reinforced his grip on the door handle. "When my call got through to Mérida, José's brother finally admitted that he knew more than he was telling before. Apparently a private museum in Boston with an extensive collection of Mayan artifacts was contacted a few weeks ago and offered a chance to bid on some hitherto unknown golden disks. The story was that they had been in a private collection here in Mexico and were being secretly sold to settle family indebtedness."

"And the museum was suspicious?"

"That's putting it mildly. Since all the major museums in the world know their purchases are open to official international scrutiny, there's no point in their spending a fortune for an art treasure that simply would have to be returned to its country of origin. A big private collector might risk it if he thought the prize was worth it . . . but even that's doubtful these days. In any case, there'd been plenty of rumors regarding these Mayan disks. It only took a couple of chance remarks by José and his unknown partner for everybody's ears to start waggling. Remember, there are a lot of interested archaeologists in this area . . . both professional and amateur."

"Where do we come into it?" Amanda wanted to know.

"We don't. The antiquities officials in Mérida would be delighted if we would kindly get out of the way. They didn't say anything before because they didn't want to raise our suspicions. And they weren't about to do anything to cause a rift in the negotiations or jeopardize their man's chances of getting those disks."

"Their man?" Her eyes widened. "You mean Miguel Melgar?"

Chris shook his head. "No, he's not the one. Although he's probably cooperating to make sure there aren't any hitches." He braced himself on the seat as the cab turned onto a narrow road marked "Aeropuerto." "Their man is from Boston ... by way of Miami."

"Kent Ives!"

Chris nodded and lowered his voice. "His gift shops in Florida are simply a cover story. Ostensibly, he's here to negotiate the purchase of the disks on behalf of the museum. Actually he's one of the best insurance investigators in the fine arts field. Once he can positively identify the disks as an authentic new find, the Mexican authorities can move in."

"I must have happened along the pier yesterday when he didn't want company." Amanda sniffed partly from necessity and partly from annoyance. "All he had to do was say so. Why treat me like a leper, for pete's sake?"

"That's what I can't figure out. But I mean to ... this morning. I'm supposed to meet him and José's brother right after we land."

"Did they arrange it or did you?"

"They did. Why?"

"What about me?"

"You had all your fun yesterday," he informed her. "I told you last night that you'd retired. You can take my car back to the Hacienda and start packing. This shouldn't take long."

Amanda's expression showed her indecision at his words. "I guess I shouldn't give in this easily but I still shiver when I remember that awful experience on the pier."

"I know." Chris's voice was terse. "Frankly I'm sorry as hell I got you into all this. It wasn't what I had in mind when I planned this jaunt."

He sounded so morose that she was unaccountably cheered. At least he still cared about her physical well-being. Better that than nothing at all, she told herself.

The taxi driver slowed again as he turned off into a gravel track which curved in front of the tiny building housing Cozumel's air terminal. Chris set about transferring their luggage to a willing teen-aged porter who appeared around the corner of the building while Amanda went on into the waiting room.

A gift counter with some silver and coral jewelry in the display case ran along one wall with a liquor shop on the opposite side. Both shops were untended but there was a hum of conversation from behind a closed door next to the gift counter. An uneven row of plastic-covered chairs straggled down the center of the waiting room. As she stood there, Amanda noted that each chair either suffered from ripped uphol-stery, sagging springs, or a missing arm. The wooden table at the end of the row was of the same vintage and held two overflowing ashtrays plus a layer of dust.

Chris came up behind her and grinned at her ex-pression. "Add an out-of-date copy of the *Christian Science Monitor* and it's just like my dentist's wait-ing room." He took her elbow and steered her toward an open doorway which faced a hangar at the end of the runway. "Come on, I hear our plane's down this way. And don't *worry* ... the Mexicans are only casual about the things that don't matter."

Amanda was relieved to find that he was right. The trim Cessna that she eventually climbed into was immaculate and came equipped with a sweet-sounding engine and a pilot who appeared blessedly professional.

After the takeoff, she was even able to enjoy their smooth flight over the gray-blue waters of the Carib-bean to the mainland. To their right lay the dark green vegetation of Isla de las Mujeres, an island still showing little evidence of resort building. The inhabitants were apparently content to live their slower life-style, letting Cozumel and Can Cun vie for the tourist invasion. A tiny ferry looked minuscule as it approached the island dock, and Amanda took a deep breath of relief that she wasn't on it. Then it wasn't long before she saw the brighter green shoal water of the shoreline and the long runway of the jet airport at Can Cun.

As they passed over the budding resort community to head inland, the gray-green of the jungle appeared beneath the wings, broken only by parcels of farmland which looked like ragged yellow-and-brown patches on the flat landscape.

The Hacienda airstrip was a mere slash in the trees but the Cessna homed into it as surely as a 747 and within minutes they were bumping along the runway and then taxiing back to a small building ... this time with a tattered wind sock on the roof.

"The car's right over there," Chris told Amanda when she'd been hoisted down from the cabin and he was walking her toward the shelter. "Head straight down the road and you'll come to the Hacienda. It's only three or four miles—you can't go wrong."

She watched him put her small bag and his overnight case in the trunk before unlocking the car door and handing her the key. "Watch the brakes ... they pull to the right, and there's too much play in the steering wheel. But if you take it easy, you shouldn't get into any trouble," he said.

Amanda slid into the driver's seat and put the key in the ignition. "Let's see now . . ." she kept her voice serious. "I turn this on and put this stick on the steering wheel in that thing called reverse ... is that right?"

"No ... first you close the door," he said, doing just that. "Okay, maybe I'm being heavy-handed but after watching you cultivate the landscape with that jeep radiator, you can't blame me."

"I promise to hold it down to ninety on the curves. Sure you don't want to come along?"

"Not on your Nelly. I'll have to see my insurance man first." His sudden grin made him look years younger as he bent over her opened window. "If I don't show up in an hour or so, send Pablo back with the car. You can go ahead and get packed in the meantime. There won't be anything to hang around for after Kent and José's brother give us our walking papers."

"I don't need much convincing." As he straightened, she added, "Take care of yourself. Remember, Kent is paid for risking his neck." His grin broadened as he stepped back. She waved and drove off, leaving him staring thoughtfully after her.

As she drove along the gravel track leading back to the Hacienda, she was wondering what Chris had in mind for their future itinerary. The least embarrassing thing *she* could do would be to go directly back to New York once they reached the United States, taking the manuscript with her. Any editing difficulties could be settled later on. Chris needn't know that she would resign from the assignment as soon as she got back to her office; any more of their tepid "business" relationship would cause her too much anguish.

The outlines of the Hacienda looked familiar and welcoming when she turned into the guest parking area and pulled up next to the jeep. As she got out of the car, the familiar bird chorus was in full swing overhead with the refreshing splash of the fountain in the tiled patio offering a soothing accompaniment.

She walked into the cool shadows of the Hacienda, smiling at a woman dusting the furniture and skirting a white-jacketed man mopping the marble steps.

Amanda found herself strangely reluctant to start packing so she wandered on to the central patio wondering if she had time for a dip in the pool. After all, she rationalized, it would be her last chance to enjoy such a treat amid the luxurious tropical surroundings.

A commotion from the far side of the patio made her smile suddenly as she recognized Junior's ecstatic form. He was plunging at the end of a restraining leash, trying to welcome her. Nearby, Guaca clung to a palm frond and squawked his annoyance.

Amanda walked over, bracing herself when Junior jumped up to greet her. "Stop it, you big lump! Now look what you've done ... you're all tangled in your leash." She patted him on the head and tried to unthread the maze. "Hold still," she told him finally. "I'll have to untie the knot at the stake. And stop washing my ear," she added conversationally. "No wonder Pablo left you in solitary confinement. You're a terrible pill!"

Her pronouncement didn't affect Junior's enthusiasm in the least. The prospect of immediate freedom was much more important in his mind and she had no sooner loosed the knot than he was wildly circling the pool dragging the leash like a caboose.

"Junior! Come here and stop that!" Amanda managed to intercept him as he veered into the garden border. "There won't be a flower left if you keep it up. It's a good thing Constancia isn't around."

Junior's tail beat a steady tattoo but the be-

seeching look in his eyes said quite plainly that he
didn't want to be banished again.

Amanda stared back at him and then reached over
to pull a rough ear. "Oh, all right, nuisance. There's
time for a little walk. After that, you can come up
and watch me pack." She shortened the leash and led
him toward the rear gate of the patio which opened
out to a service area beyond. "I don't think you can
get into mischief out here," she said, leaning over to
slip the leash from his neck once they were in the
middle of a gravel drive. "Now . . . behave yourself!"

Before the words had left her mouth, Junior was
off with another joyful yelp, tearing around her in
ever-widening circles, stopping only to sniff at the
more promising posts and trees.

Amanda noted that despite his enthusiasm, the big
dog was keeping a wary eye on her to make sure that
she didn't disappear from his sight. Apparently
Junior had no desire to return to his homeless state.
He would come galumphing back to her, nudge her
with a wet nose to make sure everything was still all
right, and tear off again.

She followed him aimlessly through the compound
of workers' huts, deserted in the mid-morning sunshine, and then left the gravel drive to wander along
a path which led away from the service area into a
grove of trees. After a few hundred feet, the path
narrowed so that Junior couldn't stay beside her but
had to bound on ahead.

The thick stand of trees on either side of the path
effectively absorbed most of the sun, their branches
allowing only dappled patches of light to filter
through. Amanda was surprised to see so many over-
turned tree trunks, evidently victims of the high
winds which coursed through Yucatán during the
annual hurricane season. Leaves from the dead

branches covered the moist ground and their rotting process made the humid air smell like a rain forest. She stopped for a moment to admire a cluster of wild orchids growing on a tree by the path and, on closer inspection, noticed several parasite air plants on the higher branches.

When Junior came back to nudge her hand, she patted his head absently before continuing down the path, her thoughts still centered on the primitive area around her. The stark surroundings and eerie quiet gave no indication that a luxury oasis was barely a half mile away.

She walked more carefully now and kept her head down to avoid stumbling on the occasional roots which protruded among the rocks on the path. Evidence of the recent rainstorm still lingered, making the fallen leaves and irregular rocks slippery as an ice-skating rink. They were especially hazardous when the path started down in the series of long switchbacks.

Amanda continued on, knowing that the flat Yucatán landscape wouldn't allow much change of elevation and hoping the path might lead to something interesting. An outcropping of Mayan architecture would be more than acceptable, although she'd probably have to settle for a garden plot.

A muffled "woof" from her companion, out of sight on the switchback ahead of her, made her pull to a stop in the middle of the path.

"Junior? What are you doing?" Her voice wavered uncertainly despite her effort to control it. "Come here, boy. Right now!" She was still trying to whistle at him when Constancia appeared on the path in front of her.

"Your dog"—the Mexican woman said coldly—"is

going the other way. Don't you have any control over him?"

Amanda's lips parted in surprise. "Where did you come from?" she managed finally.

"Down the path ... obviously." The other woman showed her annoyance by her tightened grip on a length of spiral hose dangling by her tanned leg. "I'm afraid you're trespassing, Amanda. We've restricted this path to our staff ever since one of our guests sprained an ankle on it."

"Oh, I'm sorry. I didn't realize . . . I hoped it might lead to something interesting."

"Just an old *cenote*. It's of no historical importance. If you want to see a sacrificial well, you should visit Chichen Itza. Shall we go back to the Hacienda?"

"All right." Amanda tried to instill some enthusiasm in her tone but a conversation with Constancia was the last thing she wanted just then. Chris might appreciate her finer points but they weren't apparent to another woman. She turned reluctantly and fell into step beside her.

Constancia stopped and looked over her shoulder, "Is that dog coming?"

"He's around somewhere." Amanda was staring at the hose the other was carrying. "Isn't that a part of scuba gear?"

"Of course." Constancia mockingly raised it to eye-level. "It's a two-stage regulator. Capable of giving thirty-nine cubic feet of air per minute."

"For diving?" Amanda persisted.

"For breathing *when* you're diving." Constancia was watching her closely. "I thought you'd learned all about scuba while you were on Cozumel."

"No. I'll have to try it on another trip. There wasn't time yesterday." Constancia's scrutiny caused

Amanda to move uneasily. "Speaking of time—it's terribly late. I should be back at the Hacienda—Chris is going to meet me."

"I wouldn't worry. Men never expect a woman to be on time."

"Yes, but I haven't even started packing . . ."

Constancia's eyes narrowed. "You mean you're leaving? Both of you? Why the sudden change of plans?"

"I'm . . . I'm not sure." Amanda could have beaten her head against the nearest tree trunk for her lapse but she rallied gamely. "You know Chris. He never explains anything. Probably he wants to do some last-minute checking on his manuscript in Mérida. He has a horror of any research errors."

Despite the glib explanation, Constancia wasn't convinced. "I didn't know he was working on a new book. He didn't say anything about it to me."

Amanda's shrug was a masterpiece. "That's what I mean. Writers are all close-mouthed until their brain-children are safely in print. Chris is worse than most, but I knew a woman novelist once who wouldn't even send a chapter outline——"

"Spare me your reminiscences—" Constancia broke off as a series of sharp barks cut through the quiet air.

"Oh, lord, that's Junior! He must be into something," Amanda fussed. "You go on ahead, Constancia. I'll have to find him and see what's wrong. Don't worry about my getting lost," she called as she started back down the trail. "I promise that I won't leave the path."

She was so delighted to escape the other woman's company that she practically ran down the switchback. From the tone of Junior's barks, she could tell that he wasn't in pain . . . rather it sounded as if he were having the time of his life. Probably he'd managed to surprise a rabbit or field mouse and was playing the mighty hunter, Amanda decided. Then she tripped over a protruding root and had to clutch an overhanging tree branch to save herself from sprawling. After that, she slowed her pace deliberately. She'd left Constancia safely behind and there was no sense in trying to retrieve Junior if she twisted an ankle in the process.

A minute later, she was glad that she'd halted her headlong plunge because the path opened into a rocky clearing which dropped with appalling suddenness into the sinkhole that Constancia had mentioned.

Amanda was only vaguely aware of Junior's presence as he bounded up to welcome her before returning to his prize in a nearby grove of trees. She advanced slowly to the edge of the *cenote* and stared down into the murky water below. The hole was over fifty feet in diameter with sides which sloped slightly inward, making any ascent from its stagnant waters perilous. Only the strata of limestone walls kept the pool from being a complete death trap for the unwary, the rock layering jutting out several feet to form a shelf between the water level and the top of the abyss. Over the years, a few trees had managed to maintain a foothold on the rock, but in their quest for moisture, the roots looked like talons stretched toward the water below.

Amanda drew back a step or two, unsure of the ground beneath her. Although it seemed firm enough, she was taking no chances of the edge crumbling. The Mayan maidens may have been so heavily drugged that they could face the evil-smelling green water of the sacred *cenotes,* but she wasn't volunteering as a modern-day counterpart. She shuddered and then drew back to the safety of the trail. One look was enough . . . she was happy to leave the sinkhole to the thousands of bats which reputedly lived between the limestone shelves.

Another series of staccato barks drew her over to the grove of trees. She pushed aside some drooping branches and beheld Junior's wagging derriere as he crouched over a mound on the ground. A shower of leaves and earth cascaded over her shoes as he continued his enthusiastic excavation.

For a second, Amanda thought he might have happened onto a Mayan treasure trove. The shadowy prospect of thousand-year-old bones being served up for a dog's dinner made her draw a horrified breath and clutch for his collar.

"Stop that this minute! Come out of there, Junior!"

In trying to haul the big black dog away from his prize, her foot came into contact with something hard. At the same time Junior's toenails rasped as they slid over a metallic substance.

Amanda's delusion firmed to reality; Mayan treasure troves weren't apt to be covered with a plastic tarp under a top layer of branches and dried leaves. She went down on her hands and knees to investigate, nudging Junior aside with her shoulder. "Beat it, boy. Go chase a weasel or something," she said in a preoccupied tone and did a little digging of her own.

It didn't take long to unearth Junior's goal; an assortment of scuba tanks, regulators, weight belts, and wet suits, arranged in a tidy pyramid. Amanda stared down at it, eventually brushing away the leaves and dirt from Junior's efforts before replacing the plastic tarp and getting slowly to her feet.

"Now do you feel better, Miss Stewart?" Constancia's angry voice sounded from the path. Her eyebrows went up sardonically as Amanda whirled to face her. "Don't look so ashamed. It was really rather amusing, watching you burrow like an animal just to satisfy your curiosity."

Amanda felt her cheeks redden under the other's derisive stare. "It wasn't like that. I thought Junior had found something old . . ." Her voice trailed off as she realized how absurd her premise was.

"A Mayan treasure under a plastic tarp? You can't expect me to believe that."

"I didn't stop to think." Amanda brushed her hair away from her damp forehead and moved back to the drier surface of the path. "I don't see why you're making such a fuss over a pile of scuba gear. It's just like yesterday at the pier when they were loading tanks aboard your brother's cruiser."

"Yes, I heard about that."

"I thought you had." She watched Constancia finger the chrome mouthpiece of the regulator hose she carried at her side. "Maybe you can tell me why your brother got so upset. Was it because he wasn't supposed to be there?"

"Miguel was in Playa Carmen simply because he was called back from Guadalajara unexpectedly. As for being angry with you . . ." Constancia shrugged, "you'll have to ask him."

"I'd like to." Amanda's heartbeat was settling down again after the other's surprise appearance. She decided that a good offense might be her safest move. Certainly there wasn't any budding friendship to destroy. "Too bad I won't be here long enough to do it in person, although it probably was just a case of crossed signals. If he's helping Kent, I can see how that could happen," she added fairly.

"What do you know about Kent? What did he tell you?" Constancia's words came out in a torrent.

"Why, nothing." Amanda groaned inwardly at her blunder, but floundered on. "That's the only reason your brother could have been on edge. I didn't see anything that was suspicious. All they were doing was loading some empty scuba tanks . . ." Her gaze flicked back to the mound of gear. "The same kind of tanks as those . . . the same color . . . everything. It made sense to see them on the boat . . . but here . . ." Her glance moved almost unwillingly to the sinkhole. "The only place for diving here is that *cenote*."

Constancia almost purred. "You're smarter than I thought, Amanda."

The other girl was still thinking aloud. "Chris didn't say anything about this well so José couldn't have mentioned it. Besides, the disks were in a tomb—unless they were moved later. Maybe to the bottom of a *cenote* or a limestone shelf just above the water."

"Why don't we take a look?"

Constancia's tone was so softly inviting that Amanda took an instinctive step forward before intuition made her pull up. For the first time, she recognized the glitter of hatred in the Mexican woman's glance. Amanda's fingernails dug into her palms as the aura of danger spread in the damp air, almost as tangible as the green slime of the water below.

"What's the matter, Amanda? Afraid that you'll be another sacrificial maiden?"

Amanda drew back another step, keeping a wary glance on the other woman who was swinging the regulator hose almost playfully.

"That's a sensible girl," Constancia said. "You wouldn't like the *cenote*. Nobody does . . . even the workers give it a wide berth."

"So it's a good place to hide your things ... things you want to retrieve later?"

"Or the things you don't ever intend to retrieve." Constancia's grip on the weighted hose tightened viciously. "You should have stayed in Mexico City, Amanda. Or never have come to Mexico at all. Chris has been mine all along. I don't accept competition."

"But you were engaged to José ..."

"José had his uses but once he'd found the disks, he was simply in the way. It wasn't hard to get rid of him. The same way I intend to get rid of you, Amanda. 'Accidental death by drowning.' By the time anyone thinks of looking in the *cenote*, everything important will have been removed." She inched cautiously toward the other woman, ready to swing the weighted belt if she tried to get around her.

A cold terror coursed through Amanda as she reluctantly gave way, knowing that each step brought her closer to those turgid waters. She'd have to try and fight it out! If she could avoid a blow from that weighted belt she might have a chance.

She was still calculating her chances as she lost another foot of ground. A lightning glance showed her that one more yard and she'd be over that crumbling edge. Even if she possibly survived the plunge into that horror, she wouldn't find hand holds to escape the sheer rock sides.

The malignant stillness in the clearing seemed to settle oppressively over the two women. The only definite sound was the rhythm of Constancia's breathing as she advanced in a pantherlike crouch, her olive skin suffused with excitement, her lips held apart in a rigid jaw.

Amanda's own heartbeat thundered in her ears, obscuring the last vestiges of coherent thought. "Dear god, help me," she prayed over and over.

There *must* be someone to help her . . . someone to hear her . . . somewhere!

As she took a final step back, she felt her ankle give way on a rock at the cliff top and realized she had misgauged the distance. Her lips parted in a scream that echoed and re-echoed in the deserted clearing when Constancia lunged forward.

For one lingering moment, Amanda joined those doomed Mayan maidens of so long ago; the helpless victims of Chichen Itza and all the other sacred *cenotes* who had faced their moment of truth as well— only to die horribly in their quest for everlasting life.

Chapter Eleven

Amanda's scream of terror triggered an unexpected response—although, by then, she was too dazed to realize it. Even Constancia didn't fully comprehend what was happening until she knelt by Amanda's unconscious figure to push it over the brink of the chasm.

Suddenly she was spun around so hard that she fell sprawling on the gravel path.

Chris Jarrow towered over her. "Keep your filthy hands off that girl or I'll dump you in that damned sinkhole myself—right in front of everybody."

Constancia's eyes were wild with shock but she scorched the air with a spate of Spanish as she sat up and saw the menacing masculine figures circling her.

"Take it easy, Chris," Kent Ives said from beside Amanda's limp figure. "Your girl's all right. Just fainted from shock. We'd better get her back to the Hacienda, though."

An older man in a well-fitting business suit addressed the two soldiers in Mexican army uniforms who completed the circle. "Take custody of Senorita Melgar. Once our divers go down into the *cenote*, we should have the whole story." He jerked a thumb toward Constancia, who was struggling to her feet. "Get her out of here before I let Senor Jarrow have his way. I warn you to go quietly, *senorita*," he added as she started an abusive tirade when the soldiers marched her up the path. "You're in serious trouble already. A charge of resisting arrest won't help your cause."

"When the main charge is 'suspicion of murder,' one more doesn't matter," Kent said as he watched the trio disappear into the trees. He turned back and added hastily, "Wait a minute, Chris ... I'll help with Amanda."

"I can manage ... she's starting to come round." Chris was on his knees beside her slight figure, tenderly cradling her head in his arms. "Take it easy, honey. It's all over. Nobody's going to hurt you any more. Amanda dear—you've got to stop crying." He waited for a minute and then looked worriedly up at the other two men. "It's no use ... she's in shock. We'll have to get her back to the Hacienda as quick as we can."

"I'll telephone for the doctor," the elderly man said. "There's a good man in Can Cun with a private plane. He should be here within the hour. After that, I'll escort the Melgars back to Mérida for questioning. Once our divers go down in that *cenote*," he added grimly, "we'll probably have all the evidence we need. I'm sure there's more below the surface than Mayan treasure."

The bright rays of the sun had faded to a soft gleam of gold when Amanda finally stretched and opened her eyes later that afternoon. The wooden louvers at the screened window were tilted gently to allow the maximum passage of air and overhead she heard the creak of the old ceiling fan as its blades made their rhythmic circle.

She raised her arms over her head and stretched luxuriously again, savoring the feel of the cool cotton pillowcase against her cheek and the lavender-scented sheet which covered her. Then she frowned and sat up abruptly as she heard movement in the room.

"Don't be alarmed, it's me." Chris spoke from a stance by her door. He'd made the effort to change into a fresh shirt and slacks sometime since they'd left Cozumel but his face was gray with strain and weariness. "How do you feel?" he asked quietly. "The doctor promised you'd be as good as new after some rest."

"Not bad." Amanda tried to smooth her hair and in the process discovered that she was wearing the new pajamas he'd given her. "How did I get back to the Hacienda ... and into these? The last thing I remember was walking with Junior ... then we met Constancia ..."

The sudden misery on her face brought him to her side in a hurry. "Forget about that. Constancia won't worry you again. She and Miguel are locked up in Mérida by now. He and his crew were hauled in for questioning this morning."

"I thought Miguel was cooperating with Kent."

"He got careless ... too sure of himself. And far too active for the 'middle man' status he claimed. Carting scuba tanks around in the dark of the night didn't help. When they stockpiled the diving gear out here by the *cenote*, the authorities knew something was definitely wrong! Miguel didn't suspect that the Mexican Antiquities Division was involved but if Kent had made one slip, the whole negotiation would have blown sky-high. That's why he didn't want to linger around you at Playa Carmen yesterday ... they were arranging delivery of the disks then. Kent told me Miguel was to contact someone on Cozumel later in the afternoon to final-

ize the arrangement. We know now that the 'someone' was strictly a mythical figure. The Melgars
probably engineered the whole thing." Chris made a
grimace of distaste. "They were José's unknown
'partner' in the venture, too. It was a chance for
them to make some big money—lots more remuner-
ative than selling wall hangings and pieces of pottery." He shoved his hands in his pockets and stepped
back. "Look, how did we get started on this? You're
supposed to be relaxing. I thought we'd have dinner
later on and then you could decide the rest of the
schedule."

Amanda swung her legs over the edge of the bed
and reached for her robe. "What did you have in
mind?"

He watched her walk over to the bureau and run
a comb through her hair. "We could drive back to
Mérida tonight. Frankly, I've had enough of the
Hacienda Melgar, but it depends on how you feel."
He moved slowly over behind her and spoke to her
reflection in the mirror. "Wait until after dinner before you decide. You still look like a ghost left over
from the last Mayan civilization. A fetching one in
that outfit, but . . ."

Amanda's fingers tightened on the comb as she
stared back at him. "I wish you'd stop fussing. Once
I wash my face and have dinner, I'd love to leave
here."

The lines around his mouth deepened. "I thought
you'd feel that way. It was a mistake to ever bring
you but I never guessed it would turn out like this."

"It's been worse for you." Amanda reached out to
touch his sleeve. "I know this has been a shock but
you're lucky to find out about Constancia now.
Imagine being married to her!"

"What in the devil are you talking about? José

was the only one who had to worry about that." He caught hold of Amanda's shoulder when she would have moved away. "You didn't think that Constancia meant anything to me ..." For the first time, there was amusement under his words.

"I don't know what I thought." Amanda was terribly conscious of the warmth of his hand through the thin material of her robe. "I should have realized she was lying all along—anyway it doesn't matter now. The trip hasn't been a total loss," she went on, trying to keep her voice light. "We've inherited a dog as a result of it. I hope Kent gives Junior proper credit. If he hadn't started digging in that mound ..." her eyes darkened at the memory and Chris gave her a gentle shake.

"I told you to forget about that."

"But where *is* Junior? What happened to him?"

"Pablo latched onto him when Junior was larking around on the path. Kent ordered him to get the dog out of there but it was all Pablo could do to hang onto him when you screamed. Junior almost pulled his arm off. You've found yourself a protector."

"Don Quixote with four feet," Amanda smiled. "I'm very grateful. Where is Junior now?"

"He spent most of the afternoon here with me ... waiting for you to wake up. One of the maids took him down to the kitchen for dinner a few minutes ago." Chris's slow smile brought his face to life. "But he left word that he's all packed and ready to go."

"Which is more than I am," Amanda said lightly, thinking that if he patted her on the shoulder once more, she'd reach down and bite his hand ... hard!

"What's wrong? You look strange suddenly."

Amanda gathered her robe around her and headed for the bathroom. "I *told* you ... I just need some lipstick. Why don't you arrange for that dinner." She slammed the bathroom door behind her before he could reply.

When she emerged a few minutes later, her temper had improved as well as her appearance. It wasn't surprising, since she had spent the interval telling herself over and over that she simply had to sustain a bright friendly barrier for one more day and then she could go home and weep all she wanted.

It was disconcerting to find the object of her bright friendly intentions still in her bedroom staring down at her suitcase with a puzzled expression.

"I thought you were arranging for dinner," she said with a scowl.

"I did." He didn't look up.

"Well, it didn't take you long . . ."

He waved a hand toward the bed table. "Since when does calling Room Service become a major project? I thought you could use some help packing."

She went over to drop her cosmetic bag in the suitcase. "It isn't necessary . . . oh, all right, if you'll bring over the things in the closet, I'll pack them."

He started to protest, took another look at her determined profile and merely nodded. She had finished folding the second dress when he spoke again. "Amanda, I suppose I'm going about this all wrong . . ."

She turned to stare at him over her shoulder. For a decisive man, Chris was certainly acting strangely. He stood by the closet, frowning at her poplin jacket as if it were something from outer space.

She reached over to take it from him. "May I?"

"What? Oh, sure . . ." He shoved his hands in his pockets and glowered at the floor. "Amanda, I've got something to tell you . . ."

She clutched the jacket to her breast, unconsciously adding a new collection of wrinkles to the fabric. Wait for it, she told herself. Don't let him see how much it means to you.

"Amanda, I love you. No! Don't say anything . . ." he warned when she whirled to face him. "I don't want to louse this up like the last time." He raked his fingers through his hair distractedly. "I should have known then that a woman doesn't say 'Yes' to a proposal out of the blue. It took me the whole drive to the airport to even get up nerve to ask you."

"Oh, Chris, it didn't matter . . ."

"The hell it didn't. Look, honey, don't interrupt. I've spent five months memorizing what to say . . ."

"But Chris, darling . . ."

He waved her protest aside to stare at the floor again. "I'm going to say it now if it takes all night. I know I shouldn't bother you when you've had such a hell of a day . . ."

"Bother me!" thought Amanda ecstatically. "If he'd only look up from that miserable floor, he'd know in a minute he could skip the rest of the speech."

"I thought if I gave you a month or so to cool off, we could start again," Chris went on, keeping his attention on the tops of his shoes. "But the damned project in South America dragged on longer than I thought and by then it was too late to write and explain. When I got back home, I decided to risk asking for you on this project. Right after that, Constancia showed up," his scowl deepened, "and everything started going wrong again."

"Chris, I didn't know . . ."

"I realize that." His glance finally came up to meet hers. "I could see in Mexico City that you were mad as hell. Thank god you were willing to humor me for the sake of your job."

"But all you had to do was tell me . . ."

"Tell you what? That I'd had five months to think about you . . . to want you more than ever . . . so I'd decided to ask you again? No, thanks." He shook his head wearily. "That approach wouldn't have worked any better than the last one. That's why I resolved to take it easy on this trip. I thought we'd have a nice, sensible platonic holiday in Yucatán and get to know each other all over again."

"So I wrecked the jeep . . ."

"Lord, yes!" He almost groaned. "Chalk up one nice platonic night in a hammock together. You slept through the whole thing and I could have throttled you by morning."

"At least I didn't give you any trouble in the hotel at Cozumel."

His glance scorched her. "Go look in the mirror and say that again. In that outfit you do more for insomnia than eight cups of coffee. I don't know why I even bothered to buy a room; I spent most of the night trying to forget that you were next door." He rubbed the back of his neck wearily. "That's why I had to tell you the truth now. I've thought it over and I think I finally have the solution for us."

Amanda blinked to keep the tears of happiness from showing. Any minute now, the stubborn idiot was going to give her a chance to hang round his neck and show him how much she loved him.

"Tomorrow morning we can catch the first plane for New York." Chris was going doggedly on. "I have three months before fall term. I'll find a sublet in Manhattan and court you the way you deserved all along." He grasped her shoulder and shook her gently to convince her. "By August, we can arrange the wedding . . ."

August! Did he really think she could exist three more months without him? Amanda could have screamed with frustration; instead she turned her head to the hand that was still on her shoulder—opened her mouth and bit it—hard.

"Damn it all!" Chris pulled back as if he'd found a nest of vipers. "What the hell do you think you're doing?"

"I'll tell you what I'm doing," Amanda fairly snarled at him. "I'm biting you, that's what! I wanted to see if rigor mortis had set in while you were standing there." She took a deep breath and struggled to keep her voice steady. "August!! You must be out of your mind!"

He stopped shaking his hand and shook his head instead. "I thought that's what you wanted."

"Listen to me, Christopher Jarrow," she said, advancing until only inches separated them. "I've been aching to marry you ever since the pilot reached the end of the runway all those months ago. If you think I'm going to sit around until August, you've got another think coming." She pointed a shaking finger toward the luggage rack. "And if you want proof, take another look in that suitcase. The peculiar smell in the corner comes from a dried carnation in an address book—that's what happens when a man buys his flowers in a Mexican fish market." Her voice softened. "But you'll find the rose that's pressed next to it is in pretty good shape . . ."

The look on his face as he reached for her made her break off in mid-sentence. It didn't matter—the time for talking was over. The hard possessiveness when his mouth covered hers and the passion of his kiss confirmed it. When she felt her body coming to life under his caresses, she knew their love was worth all the painful waiting.

It was considerably later that he allowed her to push back, just far enough to breathe.

"Then you *do* care?" His statement was rough with emotion. "You always have?"

She nodded, trying to blot the happy tears that dampened her cheeks. "From about two minutes after I saw you. Darling, I was such a fool that other time! To think we've wasted all these months."

He dropped a soft kiss under her ear. Then, as if he couldn't help himself, he kissed her lips again ... and again before murmuring, "It was my fault. I should have dragged you off to Las Vegas and not let you out of our hotel room for the rest of the month."

"If that's a definite offer, I'm accepting," she nuzzled her cheek against his broad chest.

"Las Vegas it is then. We can be there tomorrow afternoon. I'm not waiting a minute longer than necessary for you, my love."

"I hope Junior likes roulette."

"If he doesn't, we can always teach him blackjack." He shook his head as if to clear it and put her safely at arm's length. "You'd better finish your packing. Incidentally, I've already shoved in that embroidery stuff you bought in Mérida."

She reached back to trace his jaw with a soft, teasing finger. "Remember the one that said, 'Sleep well, my husband'? I hoped that might appeal to you."

"It did." He grinned, started to reach for her again and finally took a deep breath instead. "We can frame it for the bedroom wall. After all, you don't find a masterpiece like that every day."

"Oh, I know. I can see it now—framed in sisal—at the head of our hammocks." She smiled back at him, unaware of how lovely she was in that moment.

A sense of urgency sent Chris's resolutions flying out the window. He reached over and pulled her pliant figure back against his heart. "Not hammocks ... hammock," he told her unsteadily. "Any Maya could tell you that. Only one hammock to a family. And when you're in Yucatán ..."

"Just ask the man who owns one," she quoted in happy confusion. Then his lips came down again and she blissfully surrendered to her fate.

Have You Read These Bestsellers from SIGNET?

☐ **FEAR OF FLYING by Erica Jong.** A dazzling uninhibited novel that exposes a woman's most intimate sexual feelings. . . . "A sexual frankness that belongs to and hilariously extends the tradition of **Catcher in the Rye** and **Portnoy's Complaint** . . . it has class and sass, brightness and bite."—John Updike, **New Yorker**
(#J6139—$1.95)

☐ **THE FRENCH LIEUTENANT'S WOMAN by John Fowles.** By the author of **The Collector** and **The Magus,** a haunting love story of the Victorian era. Over one year on the N.Y. Times Bestseller List and an international bestseller. "Filled with enchanting mysteries, charged with erotic possibilities . . ."—**Christopher Lehmann-Haupt, N.Y. Times**
(#E6484—$1.75)

☐ **DANCING MAN by Edward Hannibal.** From the author of the one-million-copy bestseller, **Chocolate Days, Popsicle Weeks**—a novel that touches the most intimate emotions—a love story, moving and unforgettable.
(#W6205—$1.50)

☐ **NECTAR IN A SIEVE by Kamala Markandaya.** The widely acclaimed bestseller about a woman's struggle to find happiness in a changing India. It is the story of a simple woman who never lost faith in life or her love for her husband and children—despite her endless battle against relentless nature, changing times, and dire poverty.
(#Y5955—$1.25)

THE NEW AMERICAN LIBRARY, INC.,
P.O. Box 999, Bergenfield, New Jersey 07621

Please send me the SIGNET BOOKS I have checked above. I am enclosing $_____(check or money order—no currency or C.O.D.'s). Please include the list price plus 25¢ a copy to cover handling and mailing costs. (Prices and numbers are subject to change without notice.)

Name_____

Address_____

City_____State_____Zip Code_____
Allow at least 3 weeks for delivery

More Bestsellers from SIGNET

☐ **PENTIMENTO by Lillian Hellman.** Hollywood in the days of Sam Goldwyn . . . New York in the glittering times of Dorothy Parker and Tallulah Bankhead . . . a 30-year love affair with Dashiel Hammett, and a distinguished career as a playwright. "Exquisite . . . brilliantly finished . . . it will be a long time before we have another book of personal remembrance as engaging as this one."—**New York Times Book Review** (#J6091—$1.95)

☐ **CHOCOLATE DAYS, POPSICLE WEEKS by Edward Hannibal.** A story about today, about making it, about disaffection and anguish. Here is a modern love story told from the inside and told with an honesty that is sometimes beguiling, sometimes shattering, but never doubted. "Sensitive . . . fresh . . . Mr. Hannibal works close to the bone—and he works very well."—**New York Times Book Review**
(#Y4650—$1.25)

☐ **ELEANOR AND FRANKLIN by Joseph P. Lash.** Foreword by Arthur M. Schlesinger, Jr. A number 1 bestseller and winner of the Pulitzer Prize and the National Book Award, this is the intimate chronicle of Eleanor Roosevelt and her marriage to Franklin D. Roosevelt, with its painful secrets and public triumphs: "An exceptionally candid, exhaustive . . . heartrending book."—**The New Yorker** (#J5310—$1.95)

☐ **ELEANOR: THE YEARS ALONE by Joseph P. Lash;** Foreword by Franklin D. Roosevelt, Jr. Complete with 16 pages of photographs, this is the best-selling companion volume to the prize-winning **Eleanor and Franklin.** "Everyone who read **Eleanor and Franklin** will want to know the end of the story." —**Life.** "The story Eleanor thought was over when her husband died. . . . It is her capacity for love which shines through these pages."—**Los Angeles Times**
(#J5627—$1.95)

THE NEW AMERICAN LIBRARY, INC.,
P.O. Box 999, Bergenfield, New Jersey 07621

Please send me the SIGNET BOOKS I have checked above. I am enclosing
$_____(check or money order—no currency or C.O.D.'s). Please include the list price plus 25¢ a copy to cover handling and mailing costs. (Prices and numbers are subject to change without notice.)

Name_____

Address_____

City_____State_____Zip Code_____
Allow at least 3 weeks for delivery

Still More Bestsellers from SIGNET

☐ **BRING ME A UNICORN: The Diaries and Letters of Anne Morrow Lindbergh (1922–1928) by Anne Morrow Lindbergh.** Imagine being loved by the most worshipped hero on Earth. This nationally acclaimed bestseller is the chronicle of just such a love. The hero was Charles Lindbergh; the woman he loved was Anne Morrow Lindbergh; and the story of their love was one of the greatest romances of any time. "Extraordinary . . . brings to intense life every moment as she lived it."—**New York Times Book Review**   (#W5352—$1.50)

☐ **HOUR OF GOLD, HOUR OF LEAD by Anne Morrow Lindbergh.** The Lindberghs were the golden couple in a fairy-tale romance. And when their first child was born, the world rejoiced. Eighteen months later, tragedy struck. . . . "A totally expressive, often unbearable record of an extreme personal anguish that followed the greatest possible happiness. Mrs. Lindbergh has a great gift for communicating directly her joy and pain."—**The New York Times Book Review**   (#E5825—$1.75)

☐ **JENNIE, VOLUME I: The Life of Lady Randolph Churchill by Ralph G. Martin.** In JENNIE, Ralph G. Martin creates a vivid picture of an exciting woman, Lady Randolph Churchill, who was the mother of perhaps the greatest statesman of this century, Winston Churchill, and in her own right, one of the most colorful and fascinating women of the Victorian era.   (#E5229—$1.75)

☐ **JENNIE, VOLUME II: The Life of Lady Randolph Churchill, the Dramatic Years 1895–1921 by Ralph G. Martin.** The climactic years of scandalous passion and immortal greatness of the American beauty who raised a son to shape history, Winston Churchill. "An extraordinary lady . . . if you couldn't put down JENNIE ONE, you'll find JENNIE TWO just as compulsive reading!"—**Washington Post**   (#E5196—$1.75)

THE NEW AMERICAN LIBRARY, INC.,
P.O. Box 999, Bergenfield, New Jersey 07621

Please send me the SIGNET BOOKS I have checked above. I am enclosing $_____(check or money order—no currency or C.O.D.'s). Please include the list price plus 25¢ a copy to cover handling and mailing costs. (Prices and numbers are subject to change without notice.)

Name_____

Address_____

City_____State_____Zip Code_____
Allow at least 3 weeks for delivery

TO YOU WITH LOVE

Now the Romance of Canadian Poet Terry Rowe Comes to Life in a Limited Edition Record Album

This high quality, long-playing stereo recording includes:

- *14 poems read by Terry Rowe himself*
- *Complete original music for each poem*
- *Songs performed by a 27 piece orchestra and chorus*

And as a special added feature, at your request, Terry Rowe will personally autograph your copy of his first record album.

TO YOU WITH LOVE is an album for lovers everywhere. It's a moving emotional experience you'll want to hear again and again with someone who shares your love.

Special Offer Only $5.95 plus 75¢ postage

To: The New American Library, Inc.
P.O. Box 999, Bergenfield, New Jersey 07621

Please send me an original edition of Terry Rowe's stereo record "To You With Love." I realize there are only a limited number available and . . .

☐ I would like my album jacket autographed if possible. ☐ Send my album in original cellophane wrapper and do not autograph.

Enclosed please find $6.70 ($5.95 plus 75¢ postage) for my first Terry Rowe album plus $. . . . .(include $6.70 for each additional album).

Name . . . .

Address . . . .

State or Province. . . . . .Zip or Postal Code. . . . .

Please allow 4 weeks for delivery.